HELL HATH NO FURY

HELL HATH NO FURY

EDITED BY

SHINIE ANTONY

hachette
INDIA

First published in 2024 by Hachette India
(Registered name: Hachette Book Publishing India Pvt. Ltd)
An Hachette UK company
www.hachetteindia.com

1

Print ISBN 978-93-5731-591-3
EBook ISBN 978-93-5731-785-6

Hachette Book Publishing India Pvt. Ltd
4th & 5th Floors, Corporate Centre,
Plot No. 94, Sector 44, Gurugram 122003, India

Typeset in ITC Galliard Pro 11.5/16
by R. Ajith Kumar, New Delhi

Printed and bound in India
by Manipal Technologies Limited

MIX
Paper | Supporting responsible forestry
FSC™ C043100

Heav'n has no rage like love to hatred turn'd,
Nor hell a fury like a woman scorn'd.

– William Congreve, *The Mourning Bride*

Contents

Introduction

SHINIE ANTONY

DEMURE, SHY, MODEST, soft-spoken, self-sacrificing. Popular clichés limit women to the male imagination. For many an era, women have either tired of toeing the line or downright rejected the much-publicized ideal prototype. Every fight a long-drawn-out one: the right to be born, to an education, to cover breasts, to vote, to work, to want whom they want, to walk down a road at midnight, to use the armrest in a plane.

Poets have devoted verse to every part of her: face like the moon, lips of rose petals, hair bolts of silk. She is doe-eyed, ox-eyed, starry-eyed, lotus-eyed, almond-eyed... That's on a good day. On bad days, women have an agenda, an axe to grind, a poisoned apple to hawk. Medusa, Jezebel, Shurpanakha, Lilith, Salome, Circe. Giving everyone something to talk about.

The stories in this book explore retaliations only provoked women are capable of. Vengeance, vendetta, the silent strike, swift and lethal. Mothers, brides, girlfriends, goddaughters, ghosts, faithful family retainers, scheming aunts. Here the heroines are freely emotional, at their dramatic best, or slyly mute, going after what's owed them – respect. First, they play nice. Then. Eyes stop twinkling, the cheek stops dimpling. They curse freely, these uninvited witches at fairy-tale christenings.

The world has long grown indifferent to the sight of men losing their shit. Their aggression is legend. They go to war, slay dragons, get into drunken brawls in back alleys – they bore the world with their little-boy games. Women, on the other hand, keep calm until betrayed. Then all bets are off. A woman who plots revenge reinvents herself, reclaims the planet: 'This place is mine too.' She is not waiting for applause or a pat on the back, for the history books to record – just righting wrongs. Taking into her own hands what she is told she can't. Third person suddenly first person. Emerging like a moon from behind dark clouds to claim an entire sky.

She will tell you, if you ask her, she is looking after herself at last. Whispering 'I love you' to the mirror, kissing glass. It is called survival. Don't cross her. You don't want her coming after you. Claws out, fangs bared, hackles raised, slit-eyed, baying for blood.

Run, little man, run.

Madhavi Mahadevan is the author of three novels based on the Mahabharata: *The Kaunteyas*, *Bride of the Forest: The Untold Story of Yayati's Daughter* and *The Forgotten Wife: The Story of Hidimbi and Bheem.* She has written two collections of short stories, and contributed to the anthologies *Boo*, *Why We Don't Talk* and *An Unsuitable Woman.* She is also an award-winning author of children's books

According to her, retribution is a timeless trope. In several ancient mythologies, the presiding deity of justice is a goddess. Maat in ancient Egypt; Nemesis, Themis or Dike in Greece; Justitia in ancient Rome; Mahadevi, Mahamaya, Parashakti, Durga in India – many names, always a woman.

1

The Woman Who Lost Her Head

MADHAVI MAHADEVAN

WHEN A WOMAN realizes that she's about to be beheaded, what does she do? She runs.

I ran.

It had taken Rama Jamadagnya a moment or two to grasp what he had been commanded to do. It dawned upon him that if he did not obey his powerful father, he too would meet the same fate as his elder brothers: dust unto dust. They lay before him, indistinguishable from each other, in four small heaps. A single curse was all it had taken to reduce them to ashes.

And *I* knew – even as he was still making up his mind – that, unlike his siblings, Rama would obey Jamadagni. With that premonition, I ran.

Of their own choice, my feet took me along the narrow mud path that led deeper into the forest. Through light and shade, low scrub and wild banana groves, past a herd of deer, a family of partridges, I twisted and turned, with no guiding thought except to keep moving. I had to stay ahead – my life depended on it. This pursuit was a ghoulish reversal of how it had once been. Then he had taken playful baby steps away from me, and I, his mother, had followed, laughingly calling out, *Rama, I'm going to catch you, just you wait!* This time he was chasing me. He was hunting me down, as if I were a prey that he would hound to the margins of the universe if need be.

He was bigger than I. Younger, stronger and more focused. However, the thick vegetation was a camouflage. For several minutes he lost track of me. Yet my pace was flagging when the river appeared. The flash and sparkle of her mud-green waters through the trees was enough to give my flight a fresh impetus, a clear direction. Above the pebbles and the soft sand of the riverbank, on firmer ground, stood a single hut, almost indistinguishable from the surrounding bamboo thicket. A woman of low birth, a fisherwoman, lived in it. I had always avoided going there before, but now I made for the hut, praying that I could give him the slip.

To one side of the front door was an upturned boat, festooned with a fishing net. A pumpkin vine scaled the mud walls, on the beaten earth floor of the front yard, fish scales shone like splinters from a broken rainbow. The morning's catch lay neatly arranged on sal leaves in two cane baskets slung on a bamboo pole, ready for sale in the village market. But where was she? Where had the fisherwoman gone? The last time I had seen her by the river, she had flashed a smile and waved but kept her distance, as she always did.

I banged on the front door. It wasn't locked. I went in and quickly fastened the bolt. All was silent inside the single room. The air was still smoky from a doused kitchen fire. Murky light filtered in through a narrow window at the back, allowing me to make out the shape of things. Embers glowed in the hearth under a covered clay pot; a few utensils were arranged on a crude wooden rack; a rolled-up reed mat was propped against a wall; a piece of driftwood gathered from the shore and a string of cowrie shells lay on the floor. These were the odds and ends of a meagre existence so disconnected from mine that it was difficult for me to comprehend. Yet, for a blessed moment, I had a sense of respite. *Safe! I am safe. He will not come here.*

Before long, however, my ears caught the sound of his tread. His footfall was slower now, heavier and more measured. It came to a stop outside the front door. Slower his breathing too, it had dropped back to its normal rhythm. Next came the axe. A few quick blows and the flimsy door cracked open. He stepped in, filling the space with his massive body. It took him a minute or two to get accustomed to the dimness inside. His shoulders relaxed. He had spotted me backed into a corner. He let out a sigh and stepped forward.

'Son, have mercy. Do not kill me!'

What did he make of my words? Nothing. He was emotionless, just doing his duty.

He swung the axe up, tightened his grip and adjusted his stance. The skin on his face stretched, his muscles grew taut as he leaned back, drawing his entire body into an arc. He looked down. I stared into his eyes. They were purposeful, dispassionate, yet radiating a strange comfort. *One blow. A clean job of it. It will not hurt at all.* The blade's sharp edge caught my eye, and the illogicality of the situation struck me. The ordinary woodcutter's axe with which he was about to slay me had hung on my wall at home for years. Rama, the strongest among his siblings, would take it to the forest to bring back firewood. It was his particular chore. That morning too he had gone into the forest when his father summoned his siblings and gave them an order.

Well. Here we were.

There's nothing quite like having a sharp axe suspended above your neck to make you change your outlook. Fear drained out of me, replaced by an odd calm. Nothing I could say to Rama would make any difference to my fate, neither argument nor an appeal for mercy. After the deed was done, he would quietly go away, climb a high mountain and perform yet another tapasya... They, father and son, would go on with their lives, while I would fade away from memory, leaving not even a tiny scratch on the sheen of their reputation. I would die and nobody would know why. In those last, miserable moments of my life, the thought came to me: Why should Rama be allowed to forget that for the nine months I carried him, that it was my lifeblood that nourished him? When he left my womb, it was with that same blood streaked all over his body.

Even so, I knew that for Rama this was not at all about me. He had not judged me, his father had. The word of a father is the word of God. *Impure*, Jamadagni had called me, my body... Despite that, my other four sons had outright refused to obey him. A father's command must be obeyed, but *matricide*? It was unthinkable, they said, no matter what her misdeed. Like a king who punishes rebels in his kingdom with death, the righteous Brahmin had incinerated his own sons for disobeying him. Filicide was no sin, apparently. Rama had understood then that though his journey had barely begun, it was all about the *one* bloodline through which he was travelling and the binding loyalty he owed it. It was that which had made him realize that he had no option but to obey the outrageous command: Behead her!

Crime and punishment – when it came to these matters, erudite men like my husband always have the last word.

Jamadagni came from a long line of great rishis, seers who had won special powers from the gods after eons of tapasya. In the genealogy of these men, a sense of purpose ran strong. Their special destiny was to uphold righteousness in the world. To fulfil it, these selfless, enlightened beings strode across time and space, impervious to the constraints of both. They drew up the laws by which everyone else had to live. Those who broke them were never left unpunished.

✥

After our wedding, on the first occasion that we were completely alone, Jamadagni had unlocked a wooden chest that stood in the corner of the bedroom and taken out a sheaf of palm leaf manuscripts wrapped in soft linen.

'May I read out something to you?' he asked.

His voice was deep, eyes magnetic. I wanted to keep looking at him. I nodded silently.

He began reading, saying the words perfectly, as if they were pearls dropping from his lips. 'If the wife is radiant with beauty, the whole house is bright. But if she is destitute of beauty, all will appear dismal.' He stopped and looked at me steadily.

I blushed in confusion. 'I didn't know you wrote poetry,' I said. 'But then I know almost nothing about you. When did you write this? Was it after you saw me on the riverbank?'

A half-smile curved his lips. My naiveté had amused him.

At that time, the story doing the rounds was this: Jamadagni had seen me at dawn on the riverbank and was smitten. A few days later, he had sent an emissary to my father's court asking for my hand.

'King, consider yourself lucky,' Rishi Agastya said to my father. 'Jamadagni, on whose behalf I bring this proposal of marriage, is the scion of a line of great sages. Shukracharya, the guru of the Asuras, was his forefather. Jamadagni, too, is an expert in the science of archery. Kings fall at his feet seeking admission for their sons in his school. He is among the most influential Brahmins of all time... the right sort of connection for you to have. In my opinion, the princess *can't* get a match from a pedigree more ancient or more illustrious than his. You don't need to think twice.'

A look passed between my parents. Father cleared his throat, a sign of his nervousness. 'I am aware of the honour, Rishivar,' he said solemnly. 'But a match between a Kshatriya princess and a Brahmin rishi, no matter how magnificent his bloodline...' his voice tapered off. 'Do you really recommend it, Mahamuni?'

'I do,' the sage said. 'Haven't *I* married a princess of Vidarbha? Besides, Jamadagni's mother, Satyavati, too was from a Kshatriya family. Her father was the ruler of Kanyakubja. You are, indeed, fortunate that your daughter has caught the eye of an eminent rishi.'

'Is that so?' My father turned to look at me, surprised. 'How did *you*, er, catch his eye?' I replied with a blank look and a silent shake of my head. He raised his eyebrows and asked my mother, '*Where* has this daughter of yours been roving? I thought you were quite strict about these matters.'

'I am!' Mother said indignantly. 'Renuka is escorted by reliable servants and the royal guards everywhere she goes.'

Agastya smiled. 'I am not suggesting that she was doing anything inappropriate, but the princess does spend a lot of her time by the river. It was there Jamadagni spotted her.'

They were, all three, looking at me oddly. I felt my face redden. 'I go to the river to collect mud,' I said, thinking how boring it made me appear, as if I were a cow who had been let loose to graze. 'For sculpture and pottery,' I clarified.

'You are very good at it, I've heard,' Agastya said, with a faint tinge of condescension. 'Jamadagni spoke of your artwork.'

Father scoffed. 'What *artwork*? She makes dolls,

toys, lamps, pots. So do hundreds of women in the villages along the riverbank.'

'Nevertheless, Jamadagni was impressed by *your* daughter's skills,' Agastya said. As if settling the matter, he added in a tone of sage-like prescience, 'I would say this union is ordained.'

'Maybe he's right,' Mother said, after Agastya had left. 'Nothing else explains the rishi's sudden decision to marry Renuka. Maybe it *is* ordained.'

A rishi had seen me in passing and now he wanted to marry me. What had he, given his extraordinary vision, seen in me that captivated him so completely? Could it be love? I wondered silently.

'Ordained?' Father looked skeptical. 'It has certainly been *ordered*. You know, as well as I do, that refusing a proposal from an eminent Brahmin that has come to us through another eminent Brahmin would mean offending...'

'*Two* eminent Brahmins,' Mother concluded with a shudder. 'You are right. We can't afford to displease these all-powerful Brahmins. They are quick to anger, and their curses can be quite inventive. We must hope for the best... I'll start with the preparations for the wedding.'

Listening to them, I felt slightly aggrieved. Marriage, I knew, was inevitable for me. When a proposal arrived, one's parents decided, based on their own consideration, whether it should be welcomed or politely rejected. But I was a princess; I had expected to be consulted too. I wanted time to consider, to talk about the proposal with my mother, to feel reassured that it would all turn out well. However, everyone, it appeared, had suddenly become very busy. As my mother said, 'She may be marrying a forest-dwelling sage, but for us it's still a royal wedding.'

Even so, in the days before the wedding, she found the time to chat with me. 'You have been brought up in a palace and they may find your ways strange,' she said.

'*They?*'

'The community at the hermitage.'

'Rishi Jamadagni's mother too was from a royal household. Surely that will make me less like an outsider...'

'On the contrary, the pressure to conform may be greater.'

I opened my mouth to protest, but she cut me short. 'No, don't interrupt. I know what you are thinking. Royal families support hermitages. Your father, too, has been the patron of yagnas and we have stayed in the forest several times. However, living in a religious community for the rest of your life is going to be a challenge for you.'

'But I will be living with him as *his wife*,' I said. 'Doesn't it mean the same thing everywhere?'

Mother smiled. 'When it comes to a woman's work, the day-to-day running of a household, you are right. I am not worried on that account, you are well-trained. You will adapt too. However, in a hermitage, though the rules are stringent for everyone, there is very little leniency for women. As rishipatni, you will naturally have respect. You must ensure that you never lose it... Always remember that a virtuous woman is honoured by all.'

'All!' I echoed. 'Does that include the whole world, or only the men in it?'

She shot me a pained look. 'Men and women. In *our* world, a virtuous woman is honoured by all.'

'Just as, in *our* world, a violent man is respected by all?'

'That tongue of yours!' she exclaimed in irritation. 'You really must learn to curb it.'

'What did I say that was wrong?' I protested. 'Kshatriyas use swords, maces and bows to subdue their enemies, but Brahmin rishis merely utter curses that destroy lives. *Who* is feared more?'

'If you carry on like that, you'll invite a curse on your head on the very first day there,' she said drily. 'Don't go off on a tangent... Honour is important to everyone, man or woman. We must, each one of us, guard what is most important to us.'

'So, you are saying that a woman must defend her virtue at all cost.'

'Exactly!'

'But where does a woman's virtue lie?'

'In her body... where else?'

'Not in her head?'

'Her *character* lies in her head.'

'In that case,' I said, laughing, 'I would rather be a woman of character than of virtue.'

My mother was unamused. 'It's not like you have a choice, Daughter,' she said. 'You have to be both. You *must* be both. Once you lose your head, the body follows. Remember that, in this world, it is a woman's body that brings her shame. Do not allow either your head or your body to betray you.'

I saw Jamadagni for the first time on the wedding pandal. He appeared older than I had expected, perhaps due to the look of reserve on his face and a peculiar quality of stillness, a coiled energy, about him. It made the priests performing the rituals a bit nervous, I noticed. As for me, I found him exciting and attractive. He was tall and well-proportioned. Unlike our kinsmen, the obese kings who had been invited for the occasion, his body was lean and well-toned and his face had perfect symmetry. His eyes were a honey brown, skin pale, which in itself was unusual in our part of the world.

'I'm surprised that you find the time to write poetry,' I said to him when he read out the verse. 'And that *I* was the inspiration...'

Still smiling faintly, he returned the manuscript into the box. 'Though it may sound like that to your ears, this isn't love poetry,' he said in a pleasant but precise tone, as if mildly censuring me. 'What I quoted to you is from a sacred text composed by Swayambhuva Manu. It's called Manusmriti. My ancestor Bhrigu, too, contributed large sections to it.'

'I've heard of it,' I said, cautiously.

'Good!' He seemed pleased. 'Then you will not find it difficult to adjust to your new life. Self-control is the key to righteous living for everyone, particularly women. But I noticed that about you from the beginning, when I saw your creations on the riverbank.'

'Are you referring to the sand sculptures?' I asked curiously. 'It's just a skill I have, nothing more.'

'Your modesty is appropriate. It may be a skill for others, but in your hands, it's sheer magic.'

His approval made me glad. Though my parents had never said it, I had always felt that they thought of my love for sculpture and pottery as a useless pastime. My mother, in particular, had always urged me to learn more practical household skills. And now, I'd finally found someone who was encouraging me.

'I watched you for a long time,' he said. 'Your

single-pointed focus. It revealed that you are not like other women. As the...'

'I'd love to make something especially for you,' I offered impulsively. 'What would you like? I could...'

Frowning at the interruption, he raised his voice a notch. 'As the Manusmriti warns us repeatedly, women are, by nature, wayward. Only a woman who has succeeded in reining in her mind and senses entirely can achieve that precision, that purity which I seek in my wife.' He looked at me searchingly. 'Do you understand what I mean? I want you to attain that integrity.'

Precision, I understood, but purity? Integrity? What did he mean? He was looking at me, waiting for a response. 'I will try my best,' I said, not knowing what else to say.

'I know you will. I want everyone to see what a woman can do if her mind and body are pure. Tomorrow morning, when you go down to the river, bring a sand pot full of water for the prayer ritual.'

I gasped. What was he talking about? Even a child knew that sand was porous. Surely, he was joking. But when I looked into his eyes, instead of lightness, I sensed its opposite: a ruthlessness. It was gone the next instant, but it left me thoughtful. He was a sage with a deeper vision than ordinary men. Why was he asking me for the impossible unless he knew that it was within my grasp?

He drew me into his arms, tilted my chin up and looked into my eyes. 'And now, since you seem to prefer love poetry, let me say it. You are, indeed, a beautiful woman.' He pushed my hair back and kissed my ear with his warm breath. 'I could not have asked for a better ardhangini.'

One half of him. Love words? They sounded like that, or maybe I was eager to hear them that way.

As a child, I had always liked to play with sand. There was a stretch along the river outside my father's palace, where the sand had the perfect texture for being turned into anything you wanted. Passing the soft, moist grains through my small fingers for the first time, I had felt a current run through my fingertips. The toughness of rock, the fluidity of water – how was it possible for a tiny, insignificant grain to contain both? Yet that was the very essence of sand. It was a material from which I had learned to fashion my heart's desire. With the riverbank as my canvas, I had taught myself to draw figures with broken bits of sticks left by the waves. Circles, spirals, triangles. Once I had learned the lines, my fingers began to understand silhouettes, to create shapes. When I built my first sandcastle and the water rose at high tide and swept it away, I had laughed. I would be there the next day. The river, sand, sky – it would all be there, too, waiting to draw me in. I was Renuka, a particle, a granule, but the life force that flowed through creation ran through me too.

Sculpting living creatures was what I liked best. My creations were admired for being lifelike. Lion, elephant, bison, deer, fish, tortoise, alligator, swan, peacock and crane... as my hands shaped them, the spirits of untamed creatures entered me. I shared their world, their feral energy. I enjoyed their freedom of being.

But Jamadagni wanted something else from me.

At dawn the next day, I went to the river. My father's kingdom was further upstream. The water flow there was swift, the silt along its edge coarser, of a slightly different shade. But along this stretch it was different in an ineffable way. Walking on the silt, my feet sank in, they felt the change in texture, soft yet springy. I was fascinated by the submerged pebbles, flashing like iridescent jewels. Holding a stone in my hand, watching the drops of water slide away, I was reminded of something I had felt in the hermitage in the few days that I'd been there: a distinct vibration in the air. It was here too, in the wavelets, the sunrise, the kingfisher sitting on a rock... How often had I seen these exact scenes in the past, yet they had been nothing like this, saturated with an exuberance that rippled out from within into the world, as if the space that I occupied was the beating heart of all creation.

I knelt by the water's edge and lifted a handful of wet sand, letting it slip through my fingers, feeling its touch. Breathing in its scent. Breathing out. In that confluence of breaths, something began to spontaneously come together.

The pot created quite a stir in the hermitage. No one had seen anything like it. I watched them as they stared in silent awe. My body felt strangely drained but every cell within me was still pulsating with the excitement of what I had done. It was the best piece I had made, but I still didn't know how it had come into being. Jamadagni didn't say a word. He took the pot from me and, raising it to the sun, closed his eyes and poured out the libation of clean river water. Then he dropped the pot and it crumbled again into sand.

A collective sigh breezed through the gathering. Was it relief they felt? Their eyes, I noticed, were on him, shining with worship. But when they looked at me, it was as if they were gaping at an object: his creation.

Puzzled, oddly desolate, I looked at my husband for reassurance, at his impassive face.

'Repeat it tomorrow,' he said.

Every day, I created a single pot. Every day I filled it with water and took it back to the hermitage for the ritual offering. Word spread, as it was probably meant to, and legend grew about my virtuousness, its power to make a sand pot hold water. It earned me some respect and awe, but not as much as my husband. Meanwhile, what had once added beauty and meaning to my life turned into a mechanical duty. I never admitted, even to myself, how joyless a ritual it became. There were other things that kept me alive and for these I was grateful.

In the hermitage, time, every minute of it, was to be used meticulously. My days acquired a razor-edge exactness. There were religious rituals, household responsibilities, community obligations, the births of my five sons. Without realizing it, I had moved far away from the comforting ambiguity of my earlier, softer life. After a while I no longer wondered why my parents had stopped visiting, taking at face value the reasons they gave: old age and its attendant ills, too many preoccupations. For a time, they lived in my memory and dreams – a gesture of my father, an air of my mother, a way of smiling or saying something in that easy companionship they had always shared – and then the warmth, languor and vividness of that earlier life, too, faded away. I stopped missing my former self.

That year, spring came later than usual, but it leapt out of the ground, intent on charming everyone. Its magic was irresistible. There were mild showers, wildflowers everywhere. Birds burst into fluty notes that left the air trembling with hope. In the hermitage, too, there was a light relaxed mood. The women were easily distracted and dawdled at their tasks, children were more playful and chattered incessantly. Everyone smiled more.

The morning was already golden when I set out for the river. The water rushed past, but below the rock on which I dried myself after my bath, I noticed a large shoal of fish, lingering. I looked for the fisherwoman. She was out deeper in the water, her lower garment pulled up to her thighs, revealing her strong legs. Her upper body was bare, gleaming like polished ebony in the sunlight. As if sensing my gaze, she turned. There was a red flower tucked behind her ear. She smiled, even at that distance I could see the whiteness of her teeth. She waved. I nodded. She had always kept a respectful distance, and these were the only salutations between us, but we greeted each other every day. I knew nothing about her. She had come one day with a man who had helped her build the hut. After it was ready, I never saw him again, but she had been living there alone for several months.

After making the sand pot and filling it with water, I headed home, passing on the way a loop in the river created by a small island a short distance away. There was a grove of trees on the isle, covered with thick curtains of vine. Migratory birds came every year to nest among the trees: herons, grebes, ibises and many kinds of ducks. Their slow circular motion in the air cast fleeting shadows on the land. At first, when the shift caught my eye, I mistook it for the moving shadow of a bird. Then I looked again: Two bodies, naked, flesh on flesh. A man. A woman. He stood against a honey-coloured boulder on the water's edge, she leaned against him. As if they had just emerged, magically, from the intermingling of the rock and the river, so closely were their silhouettes merged. Entwined in a single form, a braid. One of his hands was on her breast, the other on her inner thigh.

How strange to stand naked in the open like this! Weren't they afraid of being seen? But they had eyes only for each other. Their abandon shocked me. Their ardor made my skin burn. Were they celestial beings – an apsara and a gandharva? I should not be here, I thought guiltily, I should not see this... My gaze was a molestation. But I was mesmerized. How wonderful to let go uninhibitedly, to share your body with another, to *have* something to give... Had I ever known that wanton pleasure of seeking fulfilment in another? When had desire itself slipped away from me?

I hurried on, unseeing. I could not blot out the picture from my mind. Distracted by my thoughts, the sensations they caused, somewhere along the way, I stumbled. The pot flew out of my hand, the water in it rose in an arc, fell, splashing across the front of my garment. Panic filled me; this had never happened before.

What should I do? Tell him the truth, my heart said. It was an accident. He will be angry, but he will pardon you.

But the minute Jamadagni saw me, his eyes took in my wet clothes and rage flared up in them. Turning his back on me, he walked away without a word.

Four days he stayed tight-lipped, avoiding me. Despite the uneasy calm between us, I tried to go about my daily routine. He sent word that he did not want me to fetch water for the ritual any longer.

'Forgive me,' I said, when, at last, I was summoned in his presence. 'For a moment I forgot myself. It will never happen again.'

His face filled with scorn. 'Shameless woman, you polluted a sacred rite with your unchaste thoughts. It *will* never happen again.'

At that moment I understood that my marriage, the union that I had imagined it to be, had all along been a lie. I was utterly alone. He was rejecting me. No husband, no home, no family, no commitment, no sacrifice. No God. I was bereft of everything I had seen as mine. No reputation. I would be forever shamed.

Then he called in his sons, one by one, and gave them the command. All refused to obey except Rama.

And here we were, he and I. The axe seconds away from my neck.

Suddenly, everything veered off course. Someone rushed in, pushing past Rama. I felt myself being pulled. Strong arms seized me, turned me around forcefully and tried to drag me out of the hut.

Run, she screamed in desperation, and lunged forward herself, not letting go of me.

But my feet refused to move.

Meanwhile, Rama recovered from his surprise. His arms were up again, fingers fitting smoothly around the axe's haft, as if designed for this very act. He swung it downwards. A second before my neck caught its weight, I felt, unexpectedly, a last human touch, a current of love. The fisherwoman threw herself in between his axe and me. A brave and loving but totally useless gesture of sisterhood.

She lost her head, as I did mine.

Whose blood was it that rose up in a warm spray, washing his hands and chest, trickling into a pool around his feet? Seeing our beheaded bodies lying side by side, did he feel shock? It was slightly more than he'd bargained for – Rama, my young, strong and determined son had executed two women with one blow. One highborn, the other low. One his mother, and the other? She was simply the *other*. Her killing was unintentional, regrettable, nothing more. What did it matter, the life of one woman, or even two? We are easily replaced.

After the sickening pain of the axe's blow, I knew nothing. Head flung aloft, my eyes wept tears of blood. Then the red mist began to fade, and I could see the blue dome of infinity, far at first but moving near. I was alone, adrift in a quiet, empty space, but I sensed peace. Below me on the earth, beside the dark mass of the forest, and the fisherwoman's hut where my body lay, the river flowed on, returning to its source. Just as I was returning to mine.

Beloved river! I would miss my daily tryst with her, the cool, clean touch on my skin at dawn. And she – would she miss me?

Turning his back on the decapitated bodies, he goes to the river to wash himself clean, to rinse away the blood staining his axe. The blade emerges from the water, streaked with blood. Streaming fresh blood. Puzzled, he dips the axe into the river again. The water turns into blood. He watches in horror, prays to the gods, flings the dripping axe away, but it will not leave his hand. He snarls in anger, beats his fist trying to break the blade, but the axe will not let go. It is his, the blade, the blood. For an eternity. Yet he cannot stop trying. In river after river across the land, in lake and pond and stream, in marsh, lagoon and creek, everywhere he washes the axe, yet the blood remains on the blade. It will not wash away.

Tired of fighting, he collapses weakly against a tree. Fatigue tumbles him down dark dreams. Always the same nightmare: That moment when his mother had looked into his eyes and said, *Do not kill me.* She was not pleading for her life but warning him. He will not escape, he understands now, even though he may run to the furthest tip of the land. The axe is his. It is who he is, his bloodline, his new name.

Parashurama, Rama with the axe.

Dead men tell no tales, but dead women do. Maybe because their dreams sour earlier than those of men. Death unseals their lips, bestowing an eloquence that life denied them. Like silt carried by the river's currents, their tales wash up in different places, at different times.

Jahnavi Barua is an Indian writer based in Bengaluru. *Next Door*, her debut collection of short stories, was longlisted for the Frank O'Connor International Short Story Award. Her next, a novel called *Rebirth*, was shortlisted for the Man Asian Literary Prize and the Commonwealth Writers' Prize. The third, *Undertow*, a novel, was published in February 2020 and was longlisted for the JCB Prize for Literature 2020 and the Atta Galatta-Bangalore Literature Festival Book Prize 2020. It won the Best Fiction Prize in the AutHer Award 2021 and the Kalinga Award for Fiction 2021. Her short fiction has been widely anthologized, and her work is part of several university syllabi. Jahnavi is a qualified doctor but does not practise medicine. She was born in Guwahati and raised between Assam, Meghalaya, Delhi and Manchester.

What revenge means to her: an act of retaliation that may feel more empty than the hurt it seeks to avenge.

2

The Thorny Apple

JAHNAVI BARUA

PODUMI LAY CURLED up on her side, her face resting on her clasped hands. The late morning sun fell on her face, but she didn't mind; the December sunlight possessed a pleasurable warmth. She relaxed into its embrace, drawing her knees further up, under the thin eri shawl covering her.

'Why don't you sleep inside?' Podumi's mother passed by her on the veranda. 'Sixty years old and still behaving like a child.'

Podumi considered her mother's thin ankles below the hem of her mekhela. The soles of her feet were a crazy paving of fissures. A sudden pang of love stabbed Podumi somewhere just below her left breast.

'Leave me alone, old woman,' she said. And smiled into her entwined hands. There was nothing she relished more than this late morning nap on the covered veranda in front of the house. She kept a bamboo mat and a thin cotton mattress rolled up in the small storeroom off the far end of the veranda just for this.

Podumi closed her eyes.

Somewhere, in the distance, the faint buzzing of a bee. Probably from the hive in the ximolu tree to the west of the house. Beyond the ximolu lay her land – all precious ten bighas of it. She saw the fields behind her closed lids, golden with rice ready to be harvested. Podumi shivered; the hair stood up on her slim arms. Her land! The thought of this land belonging to her was sometimes still unreal. Maybe it was all a dream, and one day she would wake up and it would all be gone like the early morning mist burnt off by the rising sun. She would be back in Mumbai, working for the family who had taken her to that bewildering city forty summers ago. How she had cried that first year! Podumi flinched as she remembered how homesick, how heartbroken she had been. After that year she had never cried, not even when that spineless father of hers had died thirty years ago. Tuberculosis had killed him, an early death mourned by her foolish mother, but Podumi knew it was the opium that had finished him off. The same opium that had prompted him to send her to work as a servant for the family that had driven up to their village one sultry summer.

'Don't you want to go home?' her mistress had

asked, when Podumi's mother had called with the news of the old man's passing.

Podumi shook her head. Let that bastard rot, she had thought. She would not send him off with the customary rituals; she hoped someone would heave him into a ditch where wild animals could feast on him.

Her mistress, who was nothing but kind, gave Podumi an entire week off. But where was Podumi to go? She knew no one in Mumbai, and the city still frightened her with its noise and crowds, so she stayed at home. She sat in her small room, where her single mattress barely fitted, and looked out of the tiny window at the sea. It struck her how much like the sea her life was: flat, featureless and headed nowhere.

There was no sea in her village, but she now had an ocean of rice, glinting golden in the morning sun. Podumi wiggled her toes and smiled.

Thock. Thock.

The sound of axe splitting wood. Michael was chopping wood in the backyard. There was no need to split wood anymore, Podumi always told Michael. They had cylinders of cooking gas in the kitchen now, and a refrigerator and a washing machine. A fully automatic one, like the one in the flat in Mumbai. All they had to do was pull out the clean clothes and hang them on the long lines in the backyard to dry in the sun.

But Michael insisted. For the occasional bonfire, he said, and for Magh Bihu. He even took across a bundle for the widow and her daughter next door. Always so generous, he was, Michael. And equally generous in bed at night when the old woman finally snored her way to sleep.

Podumi stretched under her cover. The sun was high in the sky; it would be lunchtime soon. She sat up and rose to her feet in one smooth movement. No stiffness of joints here – she may have clocked sixty years in age but in her heart, and in her body too, Podumi was that seventeen-year-old girl who had danced the Bihu with young men and women in open fields under the wide-open sky. She knew she still cut a fine figure with her long hair that grazed her hips and her slim arms, legs and waist. Podumi, the perfect name, Michael always said to her – beautiful like the lotus she was named after.

'Podumi!' Her mother's voice rang out from the kitchen. 'Come eat.'

Podumi stepped over the threshold and then changed her mind. She turned back and stepped down from the veranda. Swiftly, silently, she made her way around the house to the backyard. There she stopped, half hidden by the lemon bush, and watched her husband lift the axe over his head. The muscles on his arms and shoulders were taut as he made to swing down; Podumi felt her face grow warm.

'Michael,' she called out, in a voice reserved for him. 'Let's eat together.'

✥

In the late afternoon, Podumi and her mother made their slow way down the path that led from their house to the village.

Ten years ago, soon after Podumi had returned from Mumbai, retired from her decades of servitude, her mother had asked Podumi if she would mind taking her for a walk through the village in the evenings. After her husband had died, the old lady had stopped going out; she spent her days and evenings in the hut and the small compound surrounding it.

'I am afraid,' she told Podumi.

What is there to be afraid of, Podumi wanted to ask, now that the gravest danger has passed. Her idle, useless husband had given the old woman her freedom.

The last thing Podumi wanted was to walk around the village in those early days. The village had been agog with excitement at the news of her return. Everywhere she went, she sensed the whispering behind her back. *She has come back an old woman. No husband, no children. So what, she has brought back pots of money. She is buying land, we hear.*

They were right about the land. After her father died, Podumi no longer sent all her wages home. She sent enough for her mother to live on and asked her mistress to bank the rest. She spent very little and twenty years later, when she packed her few belongings into a suitcase, Podumi had a tidy sum in her account. Enough to buy land in the village, enough to start a new life. If one could start anew at fifty, Podumi was determined to do it.

The land was bought and a modest house built on it. Podumi wanted to dance the day she and her mother moved in. She wanted to loosen her long hair and whirl around in the courtyard like she had when she danced the Bihu with her friends. She was twenty again. Life stretched out before her.

Sweet, how sweet were the days after she started this new life. The very idea that she could do as she pleased – wake up when she wanted to, eat what she wished, sit where she wanted – made her dizzy with exhilaration. The day was hers to seize. This freedom that everyone around her took for granted had been denied to her for so long. Still, better late than never and Podumi threw her full weight behind building a new life. She hired men and women to help her plant rice, to harvest it when the stalks were heavy with gold. She toiled in the bari behind the house and coaxed luscious vegetables out of the eager earth. She helped her mother with the loom and wore the beautiful mekhelas that came out of it with a happiness she had never hoped to feel. Ah, life was sweet.

In the evenings, when the day's work was done, Podumi would take her mother on their customary walk, often stopping to visit her old friends. She visited their compounds and sat with them, attempting to catch up where their ties had been severed years ago. All married, some were even grandmothers and Podumi held the little babies in her lap and cooed to them. One day, as she carried Promila's latest grandson in her arms, she was struck by a despair that almost made her knees buckle. She put the child down, turned on her heel, and leaving her mother sitting there, ran to her small house in the fields.

What had she been thinking? How could she have ever imagined that she could restart life where it had been suspended? Fifty-two years old and she had never known a man's touch, she had never basked in that particular gaze of a man who belonged to her; she would never carry a child in her womb, and she would never know what it felt like to be called mother. She would always be alone. Podumi lay on her bed that night and wept for the first time in years. She wept as if her heart had broken and she only stopped, exhausted, when the sun rose, and the rooster crowed, and a new day dawned.

A few weeks later, the harvest commenced. This

time, among the usual faces that came to help her in the fields was a new one: a young man called Michael. He was from the hills down south and he had come looking for work. A villager had directed him to Podumi's fields. He was young – in his early thirties, Podumi guessed – and sturdy and the rest of the group seemed to like him, so Podumi let him join them.

On the second day, Podumi found herself working alongside Michael. They moved in easy rhythm, bending, cutting and bending again.

'No one will say you are an old woman,' Michael suddenly said.

Podumi straightened up and looked him right in the face. He met her gaze with a smile and, unexpectedly, Podumi blushed. Her retort stopped at her lips, and she turned around, pushed past the others, making her way to the ximolu tree.

'What's wrong with you?' her mother called out from the veranda.

'Nothing,' Podumi said.

Yet, everything was wrong. A madness seized Podumi from that day forth. She could not bear to be near Michael. She would burn with embarrassment, frustration and another urge she could only name as longing. She stayed away from him, but watched him surreptitiously; she watched his shoulders tense as he bent to cut the grain and she watched him as he wiped the sweat from his broad face with a gamusa. She lingered around the gate as the men left after work and at the sight of his strong muscled calves, a warmth spread through her body. He must have felt her gaze for he often looked up and intercepted it. When he caught her eyes, he smiled, his strong teeth flashing. There was a look in his eyes Podumi could not interpret and there was no one she could speak to about it.

Podumi was in love and she burned with it. A fever, she told herself, a disease, and like a disease it would pass if she endured it. She was mistaken. The fever grew in strength until she was no longer herself. She could not think rationally anymore; she lost her appetite and her sleep.

Her mother looked at her in bewilderment. 'What has come over you these days, girl?' she said.

'Mind your own business,' Podumi replied, but an unease grew within her. People would notice her change, if they already hadn't. She would have to act soon.

The next day, Podumi made sure she found a spot next to Michael in the fields. As they bent down, their heads almost touching, Podumi said in a low tone, 'Will you marry me?'

Michael dropped the sheaf of grain in his hands. He stood up and straightened out. Podumi faced him, feet planted firmly apart. Michael extended a hand and stroked her forearm. 'What took you so long? Of course I will,' he said with a smile.

The wedding was a large one. All the village came to celebrate this unseasonal marriage between Podumi and young Michael, but Podumi's mother danced the most. All night long, she drank the local rice beer and told everyone she came across how happy she was her daughter was finally married.

✣

'Where is your mind roaming?' Podumi's mother prodded her arm.

Podumi shook her head free of the mist of memories.

'I am right here, old woman,' she said.

'You seem lost.' Podumi's mother stopped. She gazed across the golden fields and sighed. 'I never thought I would live to see all this – this land, you settled with a man.'

'Are you happy?'

'Of course, and so proud. You have helped so many in the village. Those girls you sent to nursing school with your money, the boys you sent to that hotel training. You have done well, girl.'

Podumi took her mother's hand and squeezed it. She had very few words for love. She had lost them years ago. She put an arm around her mother's frail shoulders and put her head against her mother's for a moment.

They resumed walking and, in a few minutes, arrived at Golapi's compound. Through a scraggly hedge of hibiscus, they saw Golapi. She was sitting on a murha, chewing tamul. 'Come in, come in,' Golapi called out to them.

Two more murhas were set out in the spotlessly clean compound and Podumi settled down to listen. Golapi was an old friend of her mother's; the conversation would be long and affectionate.

As the old women talked on, Podumi grew restless. Her mind wandered again. It found its way inexorably to Michael. She thought she caught his particular fragrance on a draught that suddenly blew towards her. Clean, soapy, with just a whiff of those cigarettes he smoked, much against her wishes. Podumi remembered the way his skin grazed hers at night. Soft yet coarse, cool yet impossibly hot. She realized she couldn't live without him. Like in the Bollywood films she loved to watch, Podumi said to herself, *I will die without him.* She shivered. A knot of pain gathered in her lower belly. Could it be? No, no, she had stopped bleeding four years ago. Before that, she had hoped there would be a child. In spite of her age, she had never stopped hoping. So what if she was older. Miracles happened.

The pain was a snake slithering in her belly. Podumi stood up clumsily. She needed to get home, to her toilet.

'What is the matter?' Podumi's mother looked up.

'Nothing, you stay. Make sure someone walks you home. I am going back.'

The house was silent when Podumi got back. The lock on the door intact, as she had left it. Michael would be out somewhere.

Podumi ran to her room. The pain had eased now. It must have been something she ate. Maybe the raw jolpai she had munched on after lunch. She lay on her back on her bed and closed her eyes.

And then she heard them.

Voices from somewhere in the backyard. A man's voice and the softer one of a woman. She could not discern anymore through the shut windows of her room. She rose from the bed and opened the windows a little. The backyard was empty. Not even a hen or a chick to be seen.

The voices again, a little louder, from the direction of the outhouse in the eastern corner of the yard. A shed where they stored all sorts of unwanted things. Who could they be? Thieves?

Podumi made her way silently to the kitchen. There she picked up the da her mother used to crack open coconuts. With great care, she unbolted the back door that led to the yard and made her way to the outhouse as noiselessly as she could. There she crouched under the only window; it was shut but she could hear clearly enough.

Michael's voice. It was Michael telling someone that he loved her. Loved her? The witch. That he had married Podumi only for her wealth; that Podumi was so old all he had to do was outlive her. All they had to do was wait and, anyway, he was right next door. They were separated only by a bamboo fence. The woman murmured a reply, her voice too soft to be clear.

The blood rushed to Podumi's head. She would have called out in anger, but something stopped her. She went around, instead, to the back, where she knew there was a hole in the wall. Through it she saw them, on the floor together, limbs entwined, talking to each other as if they were husband and wife.

Podumi's heart pounded so loudly she was afraid the pair would hear it. She crept away from the window and headed back to the house.

In her silent room, Podumi sat at the wooden dressing table. She looked at herself in the mirror. Long hair open, streaked with grey, shoulders still square and stomach still flat. On an impulse, she swept up her hair and knotted it into a bun. She leaned into the mirror and examined her face. Her slanting eyes had lines at the corner, but whose didn't? Her high cheekbones still held. There were a few lines near the mouth and had the jaw softened just a little? Eight years ago, when she had married Michael, she had easily passed off for a forty-year-old. Was she old now?

A noise from the yard. Through the crack in the window, Podumi watched Jonaki leave. She didn't wait to see anymore. Podumi snatched the keys from the table and fled. She ran back to Golapi's house, where the two old ladies were still deep in conversation.

The world had changed. And no one noticed.

Christmas was approaching. Michael would soon leave for his village in the hills, to be with his large family.

Podumi would not be accompanying him this year. Although not a Christian, she had travelled with Michael every winter to his ancestral village in the hills, and his family and the church had welcomed her with warmth. If Michael was surprised at her change of plans, he did not show it; he was as attentive and accommodating as ever.

A few days before his departure, Podumi and Michael were sitting on the wooden bench in the front veranda. The sun had just set, and shadows were beginning to gather in the compound. Birds flew overhead with an urgency that signalled the end of day; some settled into the trees ringing the house, from where they called out loudly, almost petulantly.

'I want to do something special for you before you go,' Podumi said.

Michael smiled his big, disarming smile. 'What do you have in mind?'

'I want to throw you a party.' They had always had Christmas parties in Mumbai. Podumi remembered the endless cooking and baking and the eventual drinking and merrymaking. 'Nothing big,' she went on, 'just the two of us and maybe Jonaki from next door, just to cheer her up. She always seems so lonely.'

Michael's face showed no change in expression. 'Good idea,' he said.

'Tomorrow then!' Podumi laughed.

In the morning, Podumi set about her preparations. She asked Michael to get the pork; she didn't raise pigs, so couldn't slaughter one at home. Then late morning, she set about chopping and grinding all that she would need for the evening. When her mother offered to help, she refused.

'Why don't you spend the night with Golapi?' Podumi said to her mother. 'Let us young people have free rein tonight!'

Podumi's mother had never spent the night away from home and she giggled like a young girl on the phone as she talked to Golapi about it. Such things never occurred in the village – spending nights with your friends – but there was always a time for new things. She left after lunch in high spirits and waved vigorously from the gate as she climbed on to Michael's scooter.

After she left, Podumi went into her bari at the back. The kitchen garden she tended to with so much care was lush with winter vegetables and greens. She picked some brinjals and some tomatoes; they would go well together in a roasted mash. Then she picked some of the leafy greens. She could grind them with green chillis into a spicy chutney.

By seven in the evening, she was ready.

'Michael,' Podumi called out as she changed into her favourite black mekhela. Her mother had woven it for her years ago. 'Can you ask Jonaki to come? We are ready!'

Rice beer flowed like the Diphlu that evening. Podumi held back a little – she was the host and could hardly afford to lose her grip on things. Michael and Jonaki made up for her. They were almost keeling over by midnight.

Podumi decided to lay out dinner. She laid it out formally on the small wooden table in the front room. The three of them set about eating with much conversation. The alcohol seemed to have whetted the young pair's appetites. Michael closed the meal with a burp.

Podumi smiled. 'Michael, you will see Jonaki to her house, won't you?'

She set about clearing the table. In the gleaming steel sink, she meticulously washed all the plates and cutlery. She set them out to dry on the rack nearby. When she was done, she even swept the kitchen, a Mumbai habit she had lost in recent years.

When she was done, Podumi stood at the open window and looked out at her land.

Michael was already in bed when she entered the bedroom.

'You are so good to me.' Michael clutched at Podumi's hand as she lay down.

'And you to me,' Podumi answered. She said something she had never said before. 'I love you,' she said in English.

As she closed her eyes, Podumi thought of the bush growing in the corner of her bari. Her mother had wanted it uprooted but Podumi enjoyed the showy mauve trumpet flowers it produced. That afternoon she had picked some seeds from it and ground them into the green chutney. They had all enjoyed her hot chilli chutney, especially Jonaki.

Now all Podumi had to do was wait. She wondered which one of the three would show signs first. It did not matter anyway. No one would recognise the signs of poisoning until it was too late. The symptoms would be similar to that of a raging food poisoning and so it was, food poisoning.

Podumi turned over and waited for the end to begin.

Anil Menon's most recent work is the novel *The Coincidence Plot* (Simon & Schuster, 2023). It was preceded by a collection of his speculative short fiction, *The Inconceivable Idea of the Sun: Stories* (Hachette India, 2022). His novel *Half of What I Say* (Bloomsbury, 2015) was shortlisted for the 2016 Hindu Literary Prize. Anil is the chief editor of the *Bombay Literary Magazine*.

Regarding revenge, he sees it as the emotion responsible for more suffering in human history than any other.

3

Rückenfigur

ANIL MENON

YOU KNOW ME well. I am the Face. I smile and you shiver. I frown and you relax. I am your prophet and your portent; both Tiresias and Punxsutawney Phil. But once, I was just like you: anonymous and faceless, a life bracketed by mortgages and dental floss.

Till I found Indumati. Or rather, she found me.

The best way to find something is to be found. Consider the dung spider; this little parable looks and smells like dung, but watch out, dung enthusiasts! The anticipation of a delicious meal will end in learning a philosophical fact: 'like' isn't 'is', shit-eater! Compare the elegance of the dung spider's sneaky approach with the idiocy of the cheetah. The cheetah is exactly what it looks like: miffed and out of breath. It is an Aesop's fable from which I have profited. Use what you have. But friend, why stop there? Why not also use what you don't have?

I am a Kanizsa illusion: a collection of disconnected lines arranged to form a figure of choice – *your* choice. If you spot the persona and see a person, is it my fault?

'I don't know if there's anything human in there,' Indumati had said. She had been unusually calm given the circumstances.

But I speak of what has not yet happened. Best to use the narrative's missionary position: linear, cause and effect, Genesis through Revelation.

✥

There I was, not looking to be found, scrolling away on my generic phone, seated in a generic chair in the generic lobby of a generic hotel hosting a generic conference on machine learning. I had just listened to three presentations, each heralding a breakthrough. The technological future has a million faces, and each face consists of a poorly written research paper with a clever title, semi-truthful abstract, multiple authors and improbable claims of significance.

But I loved the genericity. I sat quietly in the lobby with its easy-to-vacuum aesthetic, gathering my energy and resolve to sally forth into the crowd of indistinguishable faces and interview a famous egghead or two. My editor had told me to get some doomsday predictions – the gloomier the better. Which meant I'd have to collar some senior egghead. The young ones were all malarial with optimism. They didn't believe in unintended consequences.

I continued to flick through the images of Rückenfigur paintings on my phone. Mostly Caspar David Friedrich's work. He was the master of depicting the 'figure from the back'. As always, my gaze settled on his *Wanderer above the Sea of Fog*. The corners of the screen expanded outwards and the world – this generic world – fell away. I stood on the craggy bluffs at the high edge of the world, walking stick in hand, dissolving into sky and fog and earth and nothingness, my back turned to life and all its snivels, at my journey's end. This high up in the world, the clouds had no faces. I do not know how long I was lost to the generic present but when I opened my eyes, the lobby was clearing out. My legs felt stiff. I put away my phone, began to collect my things.

As I got up from my seat, someone hailed me by my name. I turned around. I didn't recognize the face but the voice and curves and sheer *brownness* told me we had met before. She was smiling.

'Hi! I *thought* it was you.'

'Oh, hello.' She wasn't wearing a name badge.

'You don't remember me, do you?' Her smile broadened, pleased by my befuddlement. 'We met at Stanford. Chernoff's office? Are you working on an article?'

Ah, right. I had gone to Stanford to interview Professor Herman Chernoff for an article on how statistics ran our lives. She had entered Chernoff's office with some kind of 3D model, and the professor had introduced her. I wasn't surprised that I remembered that brief meeting. She fit my star signs: petite, bright-eyed, clear-complexioned. Also, curls. I was partial to curls. But I *was* surprised that she remembered me.

'Sorry, I am lousy with names.'

'Oh, relax. It was five years ago. Plus, I was just a student, while you were a hotshot journalist from McSweeney's.' She smiled at my embarrassment, held out her hand. 'Indumati.'

'Indoomatty. Did I get that right?'

'No. But close enough.'

'What does it mean?' Foreign names always had heavy meanings.

'Sanskrit version of "Selene", I think. It was my grandmother's name. Everyone calls me Indu.'

For once the name seemed to fit the person. Selene was a witch's name. There was indeed something witchy about her. I didn't want her to leave. I could chase down my interviewees later.

'Are you into machine learning too?' I asked, gesturing at the geeks lurching around us with their overstuffed laptop bags.

'God, no! I'm an artist. Mostly. What I do doesn't really have a name yet. When we met at Stanford, I'd been trying to figure out what interested me more. Science or art. Then I discovered I didn't have to choose. Now my work straddles both science and high-concept art. Actually, I came here to meet a client. I was on my way out when I saw you.'

A conceptual artist! Just the ticket to liven up a party. An image of her straddling my corpus, stark naked, and reading *Gray's Anatomy* while I played with hers, flashed across my consciousness.

'Sounds fascinating. Had lunch?' I hadn't been in the mood for company but that's the thing with moods. No consistency. 'Maybe I could write something about your work.'

'Is that a bribe?'

'Yes.'

'Okay, then.'

But as we walked towards a small bistro she said was only ten minutes away, she steered the conversation towards me. How I became a writer, my influences, et cetera. No one ever asks accountants how they became accountants.

'Actually, I don't really know how I ended up a writer. I'm not even sure I *am* a writer. What I do is journalism—'

'That's writing!'

I shrugged. 'Not quite what they believe in English departments. Or what I'd imagined as a kid. I thought writers wrote novels, period. I wanted to be one too. I studied literature in college, and amazingly, that still didn't cure me of the itch. The plan was to get a PhD and become a professor of English to support my writing. My thesis was on the recognition scene in literature.' I hesitated. *Great, just great. Keep going, Brain. Spare her nothing. Do bore the lady senseless.* 'It's kinda technical—'

'Let me decide?' She sounded annoyed.

'Okay. You know how a lot of stories, especially myths, have this scene where a character comes to some kind of realization about another? That's the recognition scene. It changes the character forever. The Greek had a word for this critical point in a story. They called it *anagnorisis*—'

'Ana-what?' she asked, gesturing me towards a group of people crammed around a joint tucked between a barber shop and an Apple store. 'Hold on, let's order first.'

The bistro turned out to be one of those badly designed vegan moral crusades masquerading as a food joint. The menu boasted about its tasteless calories with tasteless glee; the proprietor was a stringy, lean, wiry, sun-burnt immortal; the waitresses wore hemp, and their forehead bands had hashtag buttons declaring things like 'Free Palestine!' and 'Say Her Name!'

'We can go somewhere else if you like?' She sounded neutral but I sensed a test.

'And miss out on the veal? Never!'

She granted me a weak smile and proceeded to order a concoction guaranteed to be green and sluggish no matter what went into it. I settled on a faux burger.

'Okay, back to the Greeks. What was that word again?' She took a long sip from her green sludgy drink. Her eyes never left my face.

'*Anagnorisis*. Think of Penelope refusing to recognise that Odysseus had returned after twenty years. Or Oedipus learning his wife Jocasta was in fact his mother. Or the disciples in the New Testament busy counting fish rather than accept that Jesus had returned from the dead. Once they accept what their eyes are telling them, nothing can ever be the same again. Bit like falling in love, yeah?'

She smiled and took another sip of the vile-looking gloop. When a woman smiles and sips from a straw, it's kinda official. This had just become a bona fide date. One day we'd tell this story to our overweight grandchildren around a bonny fire. Marshmallows toasting in the fucking flames. *And that's how I met your grandma*.

'Sounds fascinating.'

Fascinating? Maybe. The eyes could see, but recognition was another matter. Just like that, a childhood memory coalesced, unbidden: a boy lost in a crowd of faces, searching for one particular face, dear god, for that unidentifiable safe face in a sea of fogged up, slit-eyed and smoothed out faces, nausea, collapse, blood on the face, why did the world wobble so: round and round and round the sea of faces with its flashes of teeth, snatches of hair and fluttering pink tongues.

'All okay?' she asked, sounding concerned.

'Yeah, yeah.' I steeled myself and finished the unpleasant gloop masquerading as a health drink. 'It's fascinating, but trouble is, I had a recognition moment of my own. I realized I wasn't cut out for research. Research requires a lifetime of passionate commitment to a subject. Not my thing.'

'Passion or commitment?'

Tricky, tricky. Did Grandma want comfort or the truth? We had come to a fork in the road. Did she know where either answer would lead? Surely she must. She looked like she'd had a few relationships under her belt. There are no untrodden roads in human relationships.

I liked her. She seemed honest. Not many people are honest. They say one thing, mean another. Humans want comfort, not the truth. I decided to tell the truth.

I took my time. Chewed. 'I think passion and

commitment must be the results of a relationship, not its causes.'

'Nice save. I'm not surprised you became a writer.'

We smiled at each other. She had the cutest hint of a double chin. I am a man who knows his dislikes well. I didn't like to talk shop. The conversation about work had gone about as far as it could, and it was time to talk about us. What is intimacy but the sharing of secrets? Time to shift the conversation back to her. However, it turned out to be harder than I had anticipated. Indu told me little that was really revealing. She worked in the same city as I did. She was not in a relationship at the moment. There was a reserve about her that neither flippancy nor sincerity nor humour nor earnestness could penetrate. I began to wonder if I had been wasting my afternoon.

You cannot lie to some women. Men are easy marks. But some women, they have this sixth sense. Sexist or not, that is the truth. A skill that has probably evolved from eons of surviving lying, cheating, thieving men. We called them witches and perhaps here was one before me. I had lied, and she knew without knowing that I had lied.

'I was lying about commitment,' I said, abruptly. 'I didn't quit because I didn't want to commit to a research life. I quit because I realized I was interested in me, not the research problem.' I paused and then spoke in a rush of words. 'I suffer from something called prosopagnosia. Face-blindness. I have a very hard time recognising faces. There have been times when I have failed to recognise my own parents. Crowds terrify me. It's a congenital thing, a critical piece of neural circuitry sometimes fails to develop in the embryo. I wasn't really interested in recognition in general, at least, not interested enough to keep me going. What I really needed to do was to come to terms with my condition. I did. Now I write about whatever interests me. I am happy enough.'

Face-blindness is a complicated syndrome. For me, heads with curly hair are much easier to recognise than regular heads. It may have something to do with the fact that in the critical first year of my misbegotten life, my mom had been into perms.

Indu gazed at me. How her eyes shone! So, this was what it'd taken. Idealism and confession had achieved what flippancy and cleverness had failed to do. She reached out and squeezed my hand.

'I sensed you were different, but I had no idea.' Her voice was low and quite tender. 'It must have been so hard for you as a child. And yet you are so, so—'

'Lovable?'

Indu laughed and her reserve dissolved like roof snow in spring. She'd been born and raised in one of those pointless rust bucket towns with names like

Schenectady, Binghamton and Allentown. She had done her liberal arts at Stanford, helped a forensic anthropologist on a couple of her gigs, considered going into public health medicine, dropped out, did a few data-modelling projects, and more or less drifted into a life that mucked around at the intersection of 3D-printing, sculpture and science. She was currently exploring a new material, something called morph-gels. She had sold quite a few kinetic sculpture pieces. She spoke of markets and fluctuations.

'When did artists become part of the bourgeoisie?' I asked. Suddenly, I ached to be held. I didn't care who held me. Such needs are just as inexplicable as any other need is explicable. By a woman, of course. I wasn't so blind as to mistake men for women.

'It's the other way around,' said Indu. 'The bourgeoisie are becoming artists. And why not? People can finally make a great living at art. The bourgeoisie have families. They need to be able to make a living. Now they can.'

I thought I'd kept my face neutral but apparently not. She smiled at me.

'You probably think I'm projecting. I make a good living so every artist must be making a good living. I am not that stupid. At Maryland, I did a project with the statistician Hans Rosling. He convinced me that things are much better now than they've ever been. The world rocks! Don't you agree?'

What can you possibly say to something as dimwitted as that? Optimists, I joked, were people with too few facts, and pessimists with too many.

'Wrong! It's the exact opposite!' She laughed. 'At first, I was like you. I refused to believe the time-series data Hans had collected. He must have mined a hundred different sources. Data on population, crime, TV-watching, child mortality, raw material prices, species counts, you name it. Not just for this year or this decade. The whole picture. And here's the thing. It's *all* good news. He didn't have a hard time convincing most other economists but the rest of the world was a different matter. Hans figured it was because people find it hard to comprehend time-series data. We understand size, shape and so on, but a series of slow-changing numbers leave us unmoved. He was trying to come up with new ways to visualize time-series data. It's like your thesis problem. We were trying to help people recognise the true situation of the world.'

'And did you guys succeed?'

Even I could detect the sorrow that settled on her face. 'He died of cancer before I finished my first prototype and then I got distracted. He certainly helped me more than I helped him.' She gave an embarrassed smile. 'Anyway, all I meant to say was that I stand with the optimists.'

I had to get rid of the distance between us.

'And they are not so bad to sleep with either.'

It was definitely cheeky, but the mating game is all about affordable loss. She laughed and patted my hand. 'Don't get your hopes up,' she said. 'Tell me, what do you see when you look into a mirror?'

✣

Indumati moved in with me. Perhaps I use the wrong proposition; couples move into each other. So yes, she moved into me.

She was saying something. I reflected that these days I was always catching her mid-sentence, the way one got on and off from tourist buses.

'So shall we go this weekend?'

'Go where?'

She sighed in exasperation. 'I just told you. The ballet. *Giselle* is playing. This weekend?'

I hated ballet. Ditto on opera. Double ditto on movies. Ditto double damn ditto on sports. As far as I was concerned, it was all the same thing. A bunch of individuals over-excited about something and all wearing ice-hockey masks. And ballet had a disturbing fondness for decking out performers in similar costumes.

She saw my face. 'Oh, I'm sorry, hon. I forgot. We'll do something else.'

There are some women, and Indu was one of them, in whom the Force is strong. The force of maternal instinct, that is. She babied me mercilessly and nothing would bring out that soft, melting look in her eyes than a new manifestation of my odd affliction. Like any other man would have, I did my best to oblige her.

All things considered, she was quite convenient. I think I loved her.

A year passed, then two. I grew weary of her. I grew weary of her habit of bringing food to the bed; weary of her mousy relatives (she had an endless supply of the fuckers); weary of her ignorance of her Indian culture (I'd watched more Bollywood movies than she had!); weary of the pungent odours of the morph-gels she worked with; weary of her depressing optimism; weary of her need to cuddle, her athleticism, her tea collection, her Kenyan Sheng music, her inspection, and perhaps most of all, of maintaining the appearance of not being weary.

The break-up, when it came, was rather interesting. She had been mucking around with that odorous morph-gel. Once, the sight of her shirtless and in cut-off jeans, streaked with work materials and stray curls escaping from the hair band, had more than sufficed to offset the smell of the morph-gel. But by now we had run through every conceivable perversion (ruined by her giggles), compromised our innocence (hers was the wrong kind and I didn't have any) and reduced sex to aerobics. I lost my temper.

'Dammit! Can't you do your work in a studio? The horrid smell gets into everything.'

My shout startled her. She hurried to turn off the music, then returned to sit cross-legged on the hardwood floor.

'Sorry, hon, I didn't realize you hated it that much. Why didn't you say something earlier?'

I said nothing. In general, I dislike confrontations. They take too much work. She inspected me for a few seconds, then sighed.

'Do you know you are not as inscrutable as you think you are? The most extraordinary passions flit across your face. It's almost like watching a time-lapse movie of the sky.'

I let the brooding silence build. Time-lapse this, you cow.

'Is something wrong, hon? I am sensing a lot of hostility from you.'

Her cautious, hesitant tone made me want to kick her; this was exactly the kind of junk I wanted to avoid.

'Then we must be really in love,' I remarked, forcing a smile. 'Next stop, hate.'

'Oh, please! You don't believe that.'

How the fuck did she know what I believed? Then again, perhaps she *was* a witch. I nodded thoughtfully, buying time.

She smiled (in relief?) and began to gather her tools. I disliked the smugness with which she had dismissed me. I disliked her implicit assumption that a vagina conferred on her a superior understanding of relationships. Then I realized I didn't have to stand for any of it.

'Indumati?' My peculiar emphasis got her attention. 'It's not working out. I'm bored to tears. Of you, of us, of everything. It's over. Best you clear out. Today.'

There is no telling how people react to this sort of thing. Let us not make that vulgar error that claims every emotion has a name. That gusty little *pop!* sound a bulb sometimes makes when it fuses? Her face made an expression that was that sound.

'How could I have been so wrong?' she said in a soft, soft voice. Indu sank to the floor, and much to my discomfiture, began to rock herself. I twitched in discomfort. She'd probably break into hysterics at any moment.

But Indu did nothing of the sort. Eventually, after the rocking fit had subsided, she got up and began to get ready to leave. She wrapped up as much as could be wrapped, put away as much stuff as could be put away, packed all her clothes and arranged for a cab. All this without saying a word to me. I went around the apartment to see if she had forgotten anything.

I thought it showed class to wait downstairs with

her. If she noticed, she didn't indicate it. She seemed lost in thought. At least the steady trickle of tears had stopped. She turned to me.

'That Caspar Friedrich Rückenfigur you carry about everywhere?' she asked in a water-logged voice. 'That's your entire world, isn't it?'

I said nothing. I resisted the urge to giggle. How serious she looked! As if we were in a funeral parlour (which always reduces me to helpless giggles). Naturally, the more I tried not to think about it, the more I had to. Finally, the laughter exploded from me, intense, violent and uncontrollable. She watched me hold on to my knees for dear life as I shook and shuddered with laughter.

'Sorry,' I wheezed. Then I again exploded into laughter.

'I must not let you do this ever again,' she whispered. I, of course, was immune to threats. She knew virtually nothing about me that wasn't already public information. I smiled at her. The cab arrived just in time.

'We did have fun,' I offered, after I had finished loading the bags in the cab. 'I hope we'll stay friends?'

She gazed at my face with an intensity that was a little frightening. There must be a special area in her brain, I thought, probably near her right middle fusiform gyrus, dedicated solely to processing my face.

She raised her hand, and to my astonishment, touched my face. It was quite tender. For a second, I wondered if I'd made a mistake in dumping her.

'I don't know if there's anything really human in there,' she whispered, still with that same eerie soggy voice, 'but if there is, hold on.'

Christ. What bunk. It was the last I saw of her. Good riddance.

✣

The Face is in the Guggenheim in New York City. It is deceptively positioned. One goes down a corridor and makes a left toward what is presumably another corridor, but that's a trick. The brief isthmus (representing 'Life', the guide says with confidence) is adorned with a giant Face. Perhaps the room is oddly shaped or perhaps the Face is just oddly scaled. At first, the eyes have a hard time recognising it as a face. People fall silent.

The hush holds in its small hands the universal memory of a baby's first human glimpse.

The guide points to the small footplate with some text. Classy font, all sweeping curls and duelling pistols.

Here are two pupils,
whose moons of black

transform to cripples
all who look.

'It's from Sylvia Plath's poem,' says the guide in hushed tones. 'On looking into the eyes of a demon lover.' She recites other useless facts. How the Face was built using the latest morph-gels and electroactive polymers; how a thousand different data feeds – the list grows daily – are fed wirelessly into an actuator controller; how each data feed is cleaned, normalized, scaled, massaged, and finally, transmogrified into the twitch of an eyebrow, a fold, the release of a wrinkle. Into a face.

People, the guide explains, find it hard to grasp statistical trends. Especially multidimensional trends. Graphs are too confusing. In the 1980s, the statistician Herman Chernoff had had the idea of using faces to visualize multidimensional numerical data. His idea was to convert statistical data into facial features. For example, the lips could curve with shifts in per-capita income, the eyebrows could rise or fall with population rates, the smile lines could reflect infant mortality rates, and so on. Ultimately, good news would map to happy faces and bad news to unhappy ones. The idea had been a good one but far in advance of the technology then available.

Indumati's Face was Chernoff's dream realized.

Indumati's Face? No. *My* face. She had mapped the world's state of affairs onto my face.

It had been five years in the making. But the mark of genius, explains the guide quite unnecessarily, had been Indumati's hermeneutic inversion. The Face doesn't mirror the world's data. Quite the opposite. My smile is the world's bane; my scowl, its blessing. A genocide in Africa; I grin. A thousand infants are inoculated in Bangladesh; the grin slips. The Bonobo becomes extinct; the grin twists into a smirk. Genetics achieves the first cloned Bonobo; the smirk stretches out in disappointment. The Face has all the facts, and in its misery, the world discovers its optimism.

The Face is on a million websites, its status is reported daily in the news, it's been a character in movies and it's a comedic punch line. It moves a famous brand of suppositories. There are Face-burning parties, Face-worshipping cults, and pity the poor child who bears a resemblance. Pity me, out of mercy, if not compassion.

It is very warm. My face itches. I have a beard now. I have found that people have an uncanny ability to see the man behind the disguise. There is no fog thick enough and no mountain high enough for me to hide my face. But I remember her words and hold on.

A.T. Boyle started out as a copywriter on an international book club, moving from London to become managing editor of illustrated books, in Bath, where her first stories were published. Founding and ongoing editorships of a BBC children's magazine were followed by publisher roles in Oxford, Cambridge and London. Book and magazine writing and the launch of online book reviews for a global telecoms company continued alongside managing digital awards for the UK government, and then an expansion of her arts-based work further north. Her first story for adult readers was shortlisted for an international award and launched as a dual language multimedia drama with creative workshops. In 2023, she ran the Sadabahar: Evergreen project, connecting India and England through writing, community outreach and digital. Following the death of her parents during the height of COVID-19 – their obituaries were published in the *Guardian* – she began *exObjects*, a collaborative magazine, at www.artificialsilk.org. She has co-edited the anthology *exObjects: The Art of Holding On, Letting Go* with Shinie Antony.

A.T. Boyle favours subtlety and stealth over axe-wielding, believing that what remains after a first surge of outrage can be all the more devastating.

4

The Man Who Types

A.T. BOYLE

AT TEN PAST eight exactly, the woman walked, well, it might be more accurately described as a stumble, yes, the woman stumbled into the Typing Man's office.

Aziz, who worked opposite, took time to observe this latest customer, because she was attractive, in distress and the tourists were still sleeping off their alcohol so there wasn't much else to do. The woman sat down. Aziz saw the Typing Man listen, pause, stretch his fingers across the keys and in a relatively short space of time tug the papers from the cylindrical grasp of his machine. And now the Typing Man was offering the woman the top copy on heavy laid paper and the flimsy carbon copy. The black carbon sheet he placed to the side, ready to be taken up for his next task. Directly above, two birds sang and cooed. A tram clattered. Wings flapped. The sound of a cheap spinning top was set loose on the centuries-old stones at the apron of the mosque.

The Typing Man's grandfather had set up this outdoor stall for people who couldn't write or read and for people who could do both but did not own a typewriter. A small tree, giving shade several times in the day, was a secondary but important comfort. As each customer arrived, no matter how slim or fat, Aziz would see the chair rivets strain with the weight of their concerns.

And now the woman was slowly taking the two papers from the typist, who as usual showed no emotion. The woman seemed to be trembling, but Aziz had to admit to sometimes imagining these things. Perhaps he might offer her consolation on the way past, though he was at a loss to think what this might be. Aziz's stall was populated with peanuts covered in honey, and although the scent permeated many corners of the city, his personal impact fell shorter. It was not his present concern.

He smiled.

Priding himself on being a good judge of character, Aziz reviewed the contents of the young morning. On entering the park the Typing Man had given his perfunctory wave, had noiselessly set out the table and two chairs kept in the newspaper stand's lock-up, had disrobed the typewriter... This is the place, everyone knows it, this is the time, and the clock on the tower of the restaurant will hold off until the Typing Man is perfectly installed. Here it goes, dong, dong, dong... eight signals that he is ready to start his important day's work.

What is his work? Now that is harder, for although the Typing Man is perfectly reliable in time and place, the work he does under that tree, sitting straight-backed with a typewriter that has lasted two generations or more, his feet positioned firmly on stones equidistant from the law courts and the tram stop, the kind of work he does, well, it shifts like clouds on scudding days.

The Typing Man is affected by the mood swings of the nut seller, who does not make good company, lacking the satirical wit of his namesake. Being a quietly religious person, the Typing Man would never admit to reading the works of Aziz Nesin, or to his occasional amusement at the stallholder's clowning.

Over the years, Aziz the nut seller has worked out that the Typing Man's customers are often uneducated due to poverty. They are frustrated about an unjustified fine, a certificate of birth, marriage or death, matters relating to ownership of property or land, family misdemeanours involving the police and other legal agencies who engender a fear the Typing Man must attempt to dispel in fifteen minutes, twenty at most. Generalizing, Aziz would describe the work of the Typing Man as follows: first, he listens; second, he discreetly discusses concerns, aware that the communication is within no walls; third, he generates relevant paperwork to support the cause; fourth, he charges a price equivalent to a cone of peanuts.

Sometimes a customer will return the next day or the following week, and after each visit walk or catch the tram to the ministry or mortuary or council office or housing or trading department or law courts. Aziz likes to see where they store their carbon copy. Even with careful handling, carbon smudges, and Aziz knows that this copy will be handled often.

It had always seemed strange to him that the Typing Man kept no record of the transactions. Although a faint imprimatur might remain on the cylinder where the paper was wound, Aziz had never heard of these marks being considered by the prosecution to be of material value in a case. It was an old-fashioned approach that worked to perfection.

Since taking over from his parents (who sold vegetables), Aziz had watched the Typing Man knit a priest-like mantle of confidentiality round his service. All who came to him knew that he would not break his word. But there was no denying that there must exist a record of each transaction imprinted upon the Typing Man's heart and brain which, while he is still healthy, he has no choice but to carry everywhere.

As you might have guessed, the nut seller was in awe of the Typing Man.

Moments before, Aziz had observed an abnormal gap between the offering of the two typed papers and the woman taking them.

And now the Typing Man was slowly lifting his head, not to the woman – for throughout the two heads had been angled away – but instead he was peering at the restaurant's clock.

It was the Typing Man's habit and his father's before him to register the time of each departure. Today, the difference was that the customer was still in the office; this had never happened on the nut seller's watch. Aziz noted that the fourth part of the transaction, the payment, was also missing. In spite of this puzzle, Aziz also felt drawn to the clockface.

On seeing Aziz look up, the man and the boy who ran the bottled water stand looked up too. So did the Aygaz seller. In fact, every trader in the park became mesmerized. This included the children who could not allow themselves a pause from promoting their wares; the boy selling homemade wooden tops, Murat, became fixated.

Only the woman was not watching the clock, and only she saw the prettily painted top, set to dance by the poor-looking boy, come to a jolting halt.

Why did the clock not chime its usual half-past, but insist on making silence? Even the restaurant's owner, Serhan, came out, scowling like a disappointed father until his neck ached. Turning to the stallholders gathered on the other side of the tramline, Serhan's gaze came to rest on the figure of the Typing Man, his profile silhouetted under the little tree looking somewhat different today. This could not be so, but it seemed that Mr Osman was wrapping his arms round the typewriter.

Was the world waiting for permission to move on? How could this be? Serhan felt foolish for thinking it, but he had the overwhelming sense that the woman was holding them back.

During these gaping moments many tourists passed through the park and, for the first time, the stallholders flatly ignored them. With normality skewed, roles reversed so that the tourists began to enquire about the nut coating and why it was superior to the kind back home. It didn't matter what price the scruffy boy was charging for his toys, instead they argued about how many to buy (this was unrelated to Murat's status as the youngest of nine, given a name meaning Desire to promote his tourist appeal). A student was seriously considering a bottle of water at an inflated price, though there was one in her rucksack and she'd just finished breakfast.

Like everyone else, what they really wanted was a stake in the thing unfolding. They had no idea what it was but sensed it would make a good dinner party story. What was that man doing, slumped over an old-fashioned typewriter? It looked antique and might be worth something. Why was that woman staring at him? The idea felt odd, but a few tourists were on the verge of offering help.

The stray dog Fazıl trotted up. Most dogs in the city were strays, whereas a few cats were allowed to attain a sort-of-pet status. The stallholders had come up with the name and it suited: the initial letter 'F' could be uttered with a level of venom to match any occasion. Fazıl lifted his back leg to urinate against his favourite wheel on Aziz's cart.

At first the outrage went unnoticed, but when to universal relief the woman left the office and the Typing Man painfully drew back from his typewriter and the sound of his knuckles fell limply on the surface of the fold-out table, trickety-clack, the clock laboriously came to life and tolled its half-past note.

Aziz became aware of the dog and swore and kicked at it. Fazıl was kicked again on realization that the woman had walked too far to be detained.

The owner of the restaurant burst into applause, proud of his ticking offspring, and everyone else, including the tourists, but excepting Aziz and the Typing Man, joined in. Had anyone been asked why, it's unlikely they could have explained.

Gradually, the stallholders returned to their daily business and the visitors rejoined their tour itineraries, which involved steering clear of undesirable spinning tops that were likely to choke a baby.

So here we are, safely arrived, at just after half-past eight in the morning. For the Typing Man there was no relief. He shivered in the sunshine beginning to fill the park. He felt the nut seller's eyes on him and was reviled by the sickly sweet scent coming from his stall.

On impulse, Aziz walked over, extending a paper cone graciously, some might say obsequiously, towards the Typing Man. 'My gift.' Although not wholly intended as an insult, it was taken as one. Aziz continued, 'Who was that customer, eh? Pretty girl! You know she went without paying?'

The nut seller liked to capture a distinct stance, a person trying to appear smaller to avoid an enemy, or perhaps broader in anticipation of minimizing an opponent in print with the Typing Man's help. Aziz rarely managed to make the Typing Man smile, and this did not happen today when he mimicked the stumbling arrival of the woman and the proud gait of her departure. 'New customers waiting,' he remarked, giving up and returning to his stall.

The Typing Man prickled. It was the man's insistence on calling his clients 'customers'.

In those earlier moments when others were transfixed

by the clock, the woman had done something only Fazıl had noticed. She had let the two printed sheets fall back to the table. She did not need a top copy or a carbon copy because the message burned hotly enough inside her head. It was the typist who needed to read what she had to say.

In case the strength of her message was not fully understood, both copies gave the name of the park where the Typing Man's office was located, followed by:

Dear Mr Rauf Osman,

I loved you. Now you must leave me alone because in fact I cannot trust you and truly you did not keep my confidences.

Type this: I never want to see you.

Yours sincerely,
Dilara Ayhan

Although the Typing Man had made the standard gap of line returns, the letter was not signed with his lover's name. There was none of that sweeping, intelligent style he had loved to play games with when they made up stories, taking turns to embellish every white space with exotic flowers and stamens that wept, and moons and stars that never waned.

Aziz stood and watched the Typing Man square up the corners of his newly typed sheet and its carbon companion. He tipped the gift of honey-coated nuts into the centre and screwed the four paper corners into a wayfarer's bundle. Glancing at his anxious customers waiting for the renewal of service, the Typing Man pressed this bundle, the ink rubber, sharpened pencil and pencil sharpener on top of the typewriter, snapped the ancient carrying case shut, and left. Two birds alighted and followed, soon returning to settle in their usual spot.

The Typing Man was never seen again in the park where trams, calls of traders, chatting tourists, a clock, make temporary disturbance, a place where love resides on branches.

Initially, Aziz missed the Typing Man, the customers drawn to their end of the park for a purpose, more intimacies shared closer to his rival's ears than he could ever manage selling peanuts. Aziz even came to miss the silences his neighbour would launch into the gap between their stalls, forcing a nimbleness of response, the imagined quip and banter making slow days run fast.

Admittedly, the fold-out furniture came in useful when Aziz expanded his business to strong Turkish coffee. Keeping the nuts as a sideline allowed the two perfumes to mingle, extending his reach as the Typing Man had constrained it. Now when customers stop by, Aziz has greater opportunity to judge whether they need comforting.

Recently he has taken to adopting the Typing Man's ways, setting up the inherited furniture at eight o'clock sharp, staying alert to stray rubbish, dogs, spinning tops that threaten the sanctity of his new universe. The best part is that Aziz has almost saved enough for a simple computer. When he has, he will learn to type.

There is no denying that the woman continues to haunt him. But each morning, as he rises earlier than seems natural, Aziz is buoyed by the hope that she may return, may pause on the chair opposite, may commission him to write her story.

Shobha Tharoor Srinivasan is an award-winning children's author, poet and voice-over talent who won the prestigious 68th National Film Award in India for Best Narration/Voice Over for the film *Rhapsody of Rains – Monsoons of Kerala* in 2022. Shobha has recorded voice work for documentaries, educational programmes, journalistic initiatives and audio books, and her distinct, mellifluous voice embellishes her own narratives as well. Shobha's dozen works of fiction and non-fiction have been published in India and the US, and her children's books have been excerpted in school texts and are part of school curricula in India. Shobha's writing has also been anthologized by Tulika Books, Solstice and Skipping Stones, and her essays and reviews have appeared in publications, including *India Currents*, *Bizworld* and *Scroll.in*. Shobha has been featured on radio and TV, profiled in magazines, and one of her stories was dramatized and performed by Silicon Valley Shakespeare, California. Shobha's short stories for children, *A Treasure Trove of Timeless Tales*, and her first book for adults, *Good Innings*, have been translated into Malayalam. Shobha's latest book *Look Before You Leap* explores the origins of idioms in our classical tales.

To Shobha, revenge is the long game, both retribution and redistribution, the willingness to destroy what you built with your own hands.

5

Bhavanam

SHOBHA THAROOR SRINIVASAN

THEY CALLED HER Jyothi, 'the one with light' – hoping, at least, that the name would lend some grace and good luck to the little infant. She was small when she came into the world and, what was even more disappointing, she was dark. Almost black, like a crow, people would say, as they whispered amongst themselves.

Sharada turned away from her daughter after the ordeal of the delivery. She just could not look at her newborn with excitement. With five other confinements and deliveries behind her, one more addition to the family was just that: one more mouth to feed and another body to cover and clothe. She looked around at the prasava ara. The Birthing Room. This is where, when her mother had been alive, she was tended to with such close attention. She remembered the daily oil massages before and after the delivery. Before, to prevent the stretch marks that snaked their way on an untended abdomen, and after, to coax the expanded uterus to shrink back to its normal position. She remembered the scalding hot water baths and the special foods that were prepared for her to increase lactation. She had been wrapped with the binding cloth as well in this room. Her caretakers and mother had tightly wrapped a long mundu around her sagging belly to help hasten the abdominal recovery after childbirth. There was no special attention for her this time around, though. Only the burden of seeing this infant through those first difficult months. Her mother had sadly departed a year back. Sighing, Sharada picked up an end of her sari to wipe the perspiration of her forehead, and, with resignation, undid the buttons of her blouse to abstractedly bring the child to her breast.

She still had two children under the age of seven who would have to be given time and attention. If they were not watched, Keshavan would forget his umbrella and get caught in a monsoon thunderstorm and catch a terrible cold which always led to asthma attacks, and Pramila would ignore her food so she could run out and play with her brother. Sweet little Pramila could barely keep pace with Keshavan when he skirted the paths between the paddy fields, but she toddled after him, always, wherever he went.

There was much on Sharada's mind in those early weeks of Jyothi's existence. The tharavad needed attention. She had seen the first signs of termite infestation on the pillars. That familiar discolouring on the wood was starting to show, and the surfaces of the pillars looked a little wavy, like the wood was beginning to buckle. Bhavanam was hers now since her mother had passed. She was glad that this asset had also not been given away (by her mother's usual insane generosity) to the servants and the field hands. The house was more important than the demands of another child. Besides, she was too embarrassed to have the little thing even just on her lap. After all, she had turned 40 last Onam, and soon she would have a grandchild who would only be a few months younger than this one. It would be too much to be Amma and Ammamma at the same time. Omana would have to take charge of the new baby. She would leave Jyothi's upbringing to Omana like she had done earlier with her other children.

Jyothi was six before she realized that Omana in the kitchen was not her mother. It was Omana who fed her and attended to her every day. Stretching out her firm legs on the kitchen floor, Omana would hitch up her pavada above her knees and, planting the child firmly between her legs (so that the little one couldn't run away to chase the crows), patiently made sure Jyothi had her daily nourishment. Omana could be strict with Jyothi, too. If the child turned her face away or drew circles on the food on the plate, Omana would use a stern voice. But she was usually kind and affectionate, and would even pop a ball of rice and curd into her own mouth to urge Jyothi to finish her food. And then, when the plate was clean, she would give Jyothi the piece of jaggery that she had promised as a bribe. They played and laughed together like this and passed the sultry days in the village with joy. So, Jyothi just followed Omana around, crying 'Amma' when she needed to be carried, and no one bothered to correct her.

It was Omana who dressed Jyothi and combed her wiry, unruly hair. Grooming the little girl was always a difficult chore. Jyothi would run away the moment she saw Omana approaching her with coconut oil. It would take an hour of coaxing to get her to surface from the any number of hiding places in which she may have been concealed. Bathing, thank god, was an easier ritual. The child seemed to have a natural love of water and splashing around. And recently, Omana had been taking her down to the pozha when she went there to wash clothes. It was an entertaining sight to watch thin, long-limbed Jyothi play in the water. She thrashed and splashed as if she belonged to the flowing waves.

Omana loved this little one even more than the others she had cared for. With her curly hair and darker colour, Jyothi could easily have come from her own body. She imagined that Jyothi was just like the child she was unable to have all those years ago. Soon after she arrived at Bhavanam, when Sharada sensed that Omana's body was swollen with a life beginning to grow, that life was wrenched from her. There were no whys or hows or who. No questions or rebukes. Just an autocratic decision and then that doctor in the next village with those menacing instruments. Even today she remembers the warm blood, the dull pain, the deep sadness, like it had happened yesterday. She knew at that time that there would never be another from her own birth vessel, not after that butchering assault from a professional's knife!

Omana only had the ones she had brought up to call her own now. But she was used to that after two decades of caretaking. She could still have the pleasure of seeing Jyothi through all the stages of her life, she thought. The school years with the learning, the tears, and the laughter, the adolescence with the many secrets, and then the time of marriage – a sacred, special time, when Omana's blessings would surely be sought as the young bride left home with her new man.

As the taxi rattles and bumps its way toward Bhavanam, Jyothi feels the familiar sense of butterflies in the stomach, the goosebumps and shallow breath that mark a growing sense of excitement. This should have been her annual visit to the family ancestral home in the village in Kerala. Except it has been more than three years since she has returned. These quiet summer sojourns, away from her hectic life and high-rise home in the city, are always welcome.

The tarred roads are soon replaced by unlevel earth. The car jolts on the crevices of dry mud and pebbles. Jyothi imagines that she feels the rocking irregular motion of the bullock cart that was the usual mode of transport when she was a child. Even the ground smells different here – the natural perfume of fresh earth after the monsoon rain blending with the faint fragrance of the jasmine. She sees the familiar canvas of green: the paddy fields stretched out for miles near the home like a soft carpet. Slender stalks of rice, swaying gently in the wind. She smiles, imagining that the tall, sinewy palm trees with their expansive umbrella leaves are bowing their greeting and fanning a welcome as she approaches. She can feel the strong heat of the summer sun – but rather than oppress, it envelops her in its warmth and reminds her of the cold, boisterous baths she used to have in the pozha so many years ago. She almost tastes the sweet, cool coconut water in her mouth as her eyes scan this scene in anticipation. She can smell the ripening jackfruit on the trees below her room and taste the sweet, fleshy pulp of the mangoes in the front yard. It has been too long since she visited this place of her childhood.

The sky is so blue, so vast, so peaceful here. Every bird in the sky has its rightful place. The wind whispers in the village. The breeze doesn't tease but is a gentle caress. She is going home to her ancestral house. The tharavad. This beloved place of history and memory. A serene retreat tucked away in Kerala. Bhavanam, a home of splendour and heritage. Built with the finest teak, with multiple bedrooms, two storeys high, with a wraparound porch and a central atrium, with the quintessential red-oxide floors and the beautiful, tiled roof, this house is a symbol of the finest architectural excellence in the village.

The vehicle struggles on the stony ground as it turns around the last few culverts. Does she see the familiar roof? A flash of crimson against the verdant backdrop? She imagines the open veranda where the women sit in the evenings, full of conversation and laughs as they take the knots out of each other's hair, the well in the courtyard where the servants draw water for the household's daily use. It is here, at this distance from the house, that the approach is even more slow because of the unpaved ground. But Jyothi can look for

Bhavanam, framed against the hills, from this distance. She can savour the poetic vision a while longer.

Omana knew the car was drawing closer to the house. She had seen the preparations being made for Jyothi's arrival. Ari kondatam had dried in the sun for days, and the kadumanga pickles that Jyothi liked had been stored in the large bharanis in the kalavara. But she was no longer a part of the hospitality crew. She was no longer in the main residence that she had been an essential part of for so many years. How many children of the tharavad she had fed and watered, sung to and rocked? She had wiped their tears, cleaned their bottoms, tended their oozing wounds when they fell off the mango tree. How many corners of the house she had swept and cleaned? How many vessels and clothes had seen her scrubbing and washing? The callouses on her bony fingers, all marks of her toil.

But she would not be part of the committee of staff who welcomed and embraced the visitors when they arrived on holiday. She was now a resident of the 'jail room'. That room at the corner of the tharavad where years ago Valiyamaman had housed 'prisoners' on behalf of the British. The room which still had bars on the window and was a topic of conversation and history lessons for visitors when they were taken on a tour of the tharavad. It was now the extra room in the back, close to the large unlit space where sacks of grain were stored. Did anyone know or bother that the room now had a resident?

How easily she had been 'retired'. Just like the old cows who were put to pasture and dispatched to the slaughterhouse after they could no longer produce milk for the household. One after another the 'babies' she tended were stolen, like the calves from the cows. They were sent off to schools far away and to lives that were different. She had served the purpose of taking care of them during their difficult early years. Now she had no use. She had helped with all six of them, even the rascally boys with their mischief. Yet, as soon as they turned six or seven, one by one, they were sent off to that boarding school in the hills. And then, when they came home during term holidays, their mind was on other distractions; she was not the one they came back to be with. Even Jyothi did not notice her absence.

They tell her she is 'too slow'. They say that her eyes do not see well enough to scrub the vessels until they are clean and shiny. They say she does not hear them when they call. They tell her that she misses the cobwebs on the eaves when she clears the dust. She is no longer as efficient a worker.

It is true that I have aged. It is true that the longer one lives, the more porous one's mind becomes, and the less reliable it is. But they have forgotten all the years of back-breaking work I gave to the residents of Bhavanam. They sucked my youth dry and then threw me away like the mango pits that littered the kitchen when I used to clean the house. Now that my joints have swollen and I cannot squat on the floor, they have erased me from their minds. Now that there are young and more swift-footed staff to deal with their demands, they give me little thought.

Jyothi leans back against the plastic seat of the car. Bhavanam will soon be hers. Sharada has been a presiding matriarch, holding sway as a monarch in a palace, for eight decades, but now the time has come for the daughters to take charge. The boys are all well settled. Pramila is wrapped up in her academic life. Jyothi knows that Pramila has little care for house or wealth. Bhavanam, according to tradition, will belong to a daughter; it will be Jyothi's.

How she had missed it all when she first left Bhavanam for the hills. But the friends and frolic of boarding school had supplanted the brief pining for her playful childhood with Omana. In fact, her trips back to the village were infrequent while she was in school. She was soon caught up in the newness and the excitement of a different life. There were field trips that kept her away, and twice she did not return to the tharavad because there were family visits to her brothers in the US during school holidays. And then later, in high school, there were internships in Bombay. She had mostly forgotten her Malayalam by then. She was now a trendy city girl. Along with her early childhood, she had forgotten Omana as well. The household staff were just people to attend to her needs when she paid the village home a visit. Today, she is Jyothi Menon, Senior Program Manager at an MNC in the nation's capital.

The wheels of the taxi heave and groan its protest as it rumbles slowly forward – the vision of this tranquil retreat, framed against the rolling hills of the Western Ghats and the vast green fields of rice, will remain a vision a while longer as the car turns at the culvert for the last bend approaching the house.

There is more than one way to enter the present from the past. They think I have lost my mind. That I have no skills or the power to tell the stories of the family that I served. But I know their secrets. I was there in the kitchen when Gopal met Jyothi in the room at the back. I heard the amorous whispers and stifled giggles. I wanted to barge in there and tell that boy off. I wanted to send him away with shouts and threats of serious punishment. But what position did I have? I was no longer Amma. That dusky, beautiful girl that I raised as my own with such love barely spoke to me or looked in my direction.

I know other things as well. I know about the incessant needs of the woman of the house. That tired man who came home after his long day supervising the paddy staff had to make sure he kept his wife happy at night. I heard the noises from the bedroom. Her loud moans. The humping and heaving. I heard her ask for more. Again, and again. Sharada's appetite was enormous. No wonder he left the world as early as he did. And then there is Keshavan. Just like his mother. All take and no give. No surprise that Keshavan is the man he is. I know it was he who 'befriended' the girls in the house next door. One by one, he seduced them and deflowered them for his pleasure. I could see that the girls were smitten by his sweet talk and songs of love. They hung on to every word of his colourful stories – full of descriptions of the places he had seen. They laughed at his jokes and allowed his fingers to stray. Such a precocious fellow. He had a way with the girls from when he was in high school. They were all older than him, but that didn't seem to matter to those girls. And it didn't matter to Keshavan either. That boy didn't care about age. They cooked him his favourite mathi fry and kootucurries, and when the time came, they warmed his bed and taught him how to be a man. I knew that the coupling was not in a room, that pushing and rutting happened elsewhere. The attic, the fields, the soft earth behind the cowshed – all these places have stories to tell.

But what was the point of it all? Did any of it matter? Only to the women who imagined themselves in love. They cried in corners when he left. And then, one by one, they were packed off to other men and other lives. Keshavan just gathered his trophies and moved on. And, of course, when it was time for his marriage, the tharavatamma, Sharada, forged the necessary appropriate alliance. My Jyothi too was sent off. The village was not where Sharada's progeny would live their lives.

✣

The first thing that you notice about a burning house is not that it is burning, but that it is changing colour before your eyes.

Smoke, light and white, drifts toward her. A haze to start, then billowing fumes darkening to a sooty black as they gather pieces of the home. The flames are everywhere; the red roof is glowing in the evening light, and it is on fire. Those heavy teak carved doors and windows that looked down at the jackfruit and mango for so many years are on fire. Fire is coming out of the house through various crevices. A shower of sparks. Shooting flames. The crackle and spit of explosive sounds. The scorching heat like from a furnace. Acrid smells in the air.

Jyothi sees flames rising up in the air with the wind. Like they are trying to catch something else on fire. Perhaps all those memories.

The laughter and the tears are swept up in smoke and ash. It takes a family many years to build a house and it takes nature only a few minutes to destroy it, and their dreams with it.

Bhavanam lights up against the green paddy. That portrait of perfection now burnished with the blazing colours of a roaring fire. Flames lick the walls. Flames dance over the mittam that saw Onams and kalyanams. Fire leaps into life, remembering the little ones that grew up inside these walls. Fire, full of light, encircles Jyothi like the embrace that awaited her arrival.

How do I imagine the lives of those I love? Perhaps I can get closer to them if I show them what I once was. Sometimes the thin veil confusing my mind lifts and I can see clearly. I am now kanmashi-filled eyes and long black tresses. I am the timid girl full of hope brought by my uncle to this tharavad after my parents left the world. Only sixteen. Still a child some would say. But they saw my strength and youthful energy. My multicoloured bangles twinkled in the sunlight and tinkled against each other as I walked into my new home, my red pavada rustling in the breeze.

The faces of those I loved are before me. Small innocent faces, laughing and shrieking as we play. Jyothi and me in the pozha. The sound of feet running against the fronds of the paddy fields. But the images are darkening. Shapes and forms change. They are contorted now as visages of derision and scowls. I feel the flesh torn from me. I feel the harshness of discard.

The cow in the barn moos in distress, breaking the silence. The breeze makes the flames leap and dance, erasing the darkness of my mind.

I will start another chapter. I am now the Amma of the tharavad. I, Omana, the matriarch. I built the life within its walls. I am the keeper of Bhavanam's stories. This is my home. The palm trees bordering the far end of the rice fields are darkening in the shadowy embrace of the approaching dusk. Soon, a new dawn will awaken. I feel the invitation in the countryside. I am coming home.

Anuja Chandramouli is a bestselling author and new-age Indian classicist who has published 12 books across the mythology, historical fiction and fantasy genres, with varying degrees of success. Her debut novel, *Arjuna: Saga of a Pandava Warrior-Prince*, was named as one of the top 5 sellers in Indian Writing (2012) by Amazon India. Her book *Mohini: The Enchantress* was awarded the AutHer award in the Popular Choice category (2021). The author feels these minor accomplishments coupled with the blue tick Instagram in its infinite wisdom bestowed upon her validate her entire existence, because she is a bit of a masochist and more than a little pathetic, though she wouldn't admit as much in a billion years. If she were inclined to brag about even more minor achievements, she would want it mentioned that she is a TEDx speaker, storyteller, content creator, columnist, trained Bharatnatyam dancer, dog parent, and mum to two snarky teen daughters who think she is cringe as well as lame. She can also do a headstand with only minimal risk to life and limb.

As far as Anuja is concerned, revenge, with murder and mayhem thrown in for good measure, works best in the artistic space, as you can get away with it, and might even win an award or two if you play it just right.

6

Wretched

ANUJA CHANDRAMOULI

SHE FELT MISERABLE. It was how she felt on the best of days, so it would be accurate to say that she felt more wretchedly miserable than was usual even for her. It wasn't only the strands of silver that grew atop her head in an increasingly dense thatch, the burgeoning waistline from all the comfort-eating she was prone to, her non-existent life or career prospects at the ripe old age of thirty-something or even the fact that she lived with her evil grandmother in a shoebox on a desolate stretch of a shitty little town which might as well have been nowhere.

The achy sinuses, scratchy throat, leaky nose, throbbing temples, rising temperature and sneezing fits that plagued her as she sat hunched miserably over her laptop on a wet and foul night, struggling to find the words that were hopelessly lost to her, for the manuscript she had been working on, for what felt like a century and a half, might have been the obvious cause for the heightened sense of angst, but there was more. It was the encroaching sense of hopelessness that had crept up on her, and she no longer had her grandiose, extremely improbable dreams to fend it off.

Ordinarily, she tried not to encourage her tendency to feel sorry for herself, but since she was suffering from a wicked bout of the flu (could it be some mutant strain of the dreaded SARS-CoV-2 virus that was likely to wipe out all of humanity in a single fell blow?), she had given herself permission to wallow in a bottomless abyss of misery and self-pity. So, she ate everything in sight (not even the bubonic plague could curb her appetite it seemed), swallowed the self-prescribed antibiotic and paracetamol with cough syrup while pondering morosely about lost dreams, unfinished manuscripts and a wasted life that might as well have been flushed down the toilet from the get-go.

Such dreams they had been... before they had been relegated unceremoniously to the trash heap of her existence. Big, beautiful dreams that featured her living a glorious life and loving every single moment of it. In the realms of fantasy, she was a fabulously wealthy, award-winning, bestselling author who never ran out of words or ideas, living in an opulent beach house exactly like the one Tony Stark had in *Iron Man*.

There were lovers aplenty, in la-la land, of the sporty as well as arty variety. Some of them had even been resurrected from the dead or brought to life from fiction to fuel her sex-soaked fantasies. Alexander the Great, Julius Caesar, Scipio Africanus, Richard Burton, Oscar Wilde, Raja Raja Chozhan, Prithviraj Chauhan, Kobe Bryant, Rhett Butler, Aragorn, Legolas, Sherlock Holmes… how she had loved in those dreams! And been loved back! It was all very intimate, memorable and simply marvellous. Sometimes it was nasty. Entirely devoid of anything but pornographic value. A fornication fest of orgiastic bliss with her afloat on a sea of seminal fluids. Which was even better.

She was effortlessly skinny in her dreams and always impeccably groomed. She travelled the length and breadth of the world on carefully curated book tours, where her admirers hung on every word she uttered, panted for autographs and clicked selfies with her. Publishing houses fought over the rights to her books and the chance to enrich her even further. Ivy League colleges begged her to address their students, tempting her with indecently fat cheques. Studio executives began a bidding war to buy the movie rights to her books and begged her to star in them.

Of course, she acceded. But only after they had agreed to pay her an arm and a leg. Soon she was accepting the Academy Award and delivering a witty speech while togged out in haute couture, specially designed for her by some hotshot, and accessorized with some classy Cartier diamonds and those high-heeled shoes made by sadistic men who believe walking should be a painful experience and running next to impossible.

It wasn't always about books, money, fame, art, or sex. Sometimes, she was a criminal psychologist/profiler who put serial killers behind bars. Or an explorer and intrepid traveller like Marco Polo or Ibn Battuta, journeying to the remote reaches of the cosmos and seeing all the marvels there were to see.

In those mesmerizing dreams, where she could be anything and everything, she sang, danced, acted her heart out, and made love with wildly fascinating people. Sometimes the fabulous folks who wandered into her dreams became her closest friends who held her in their arms and listened to whatever shit popped into her head and spilled out of her mouth. They had the best conversations about everything and nothing over steaming cups of milky coffee and cake. She went wherever her whims led her and was delirious with joy. For, in her dreams, she was never afraid. And always happier than she could bear.

If only she could have really lived in her dreams! But it was hard to carry on dreaming. Especially when reality with its unvarnished ugliness forced its way into her system like an unwelcome virus and refused to get lost. Thanks, or no thanks to the heartbreaking beauty of her dreams, her singularly dismal existence had become even more so and there was no escaping it. Slowly but inexorably, she sank into a quagmire of depression and despair.

Past hurts and losses resurfaced to keep her company in her sorrow, and she kept the painful memories close. She had lost both her parents while still a child. Her wicked grandmother had kindly taken her in. Only to hold her captive forever more in the shoebox, where the old bat had resided ever since her own husband had kicked the bucket a long time ago. The harridan had never forgiven her only son for marrying against her wishes, compounding his error by dying young and foisting the fruit of his loins on her. Grandmother had hated her daughter-in-law, whom she considered ill-omened. Since she was an uglier version of her mom, Grandma dearest hated her too.

She continued her studies in a cloistered all-girls school, chosen and grudgingly paid for by the matriarch. Later, grumbling incessantly, Grandmother shelled out for a seat in an all-girls college, the only one in their god-awful town. She used to dream of running away to greener pastures with a handsome stranger but none crossed her path. Not even sleazy slimeballs, would-be rapists or others of that ilk.

The belligerent bitch was fully committed to preserving her virtue, so there were no men in her life. Unless you counted the crusty old chauffeur who was loyal to the old fart, and her ancient manservant, who hoicked up his lungi to expose his colourful underwear and spent the days pretending to sweep and swab the shoebox when, in reality, he did little more than sneakily smoke his beedis, hawk up phlegm and spit it out in a grotesque projectile onto their veggie patch.

Her life would have been even more pathetic if it hadn't been for her late father's collection of books, carefully preserved by his grouch of a mum. The nag encouraged her to read to her heart's content and even ensured that there was a steady supply of snacks for her to munch on as she swam across entire oceans of words. Only belatedly did she realize that the harpy had figured that chubby girls with their noses buried in books were less likely to elope with the first member of the opposite sex who was ready, willing and able. Too bad she wasn't a lesbian. It would have given the old crone the cardiac arrest she so richly deserved!

There had been a few marriage proposals. But the tyrant had rejected them all. Even the somewhat decent-looking neurosurgeon who lived in Switzerland. Thereby depriving her of a lifetime spent stuffing her face with gourmet chocolate and getting hopped up on sugar and fondue while gambolling on snow-clad mountain slopes. She had never forgiven her for it.

How dare the old crow reject a neurosurgeon from Switzerland? Everyone said it was because her evil grandmother had gotten used to bossing her around and needed her granddaughter around to nurse her through the advanced stages of old age, decrepitude, and the rest of it, till death did them part. She had a bad feeling that the ancient one would outlive them all. Even if the apocalypse struck and took everything, including the cockroaches, the ornery ogress would live on forever, parasitically feeding on anyone and everything in her immediate vicinity.

Admittedly, the good doctor had been the only good prospect. The rest were mostly losers with bloodshot eyes, balding heads and bulging paunches. She felt only mildly bad for appraising them on the strength of their physical attributes, given her own shortcomings in that department.

The offers dried up when word got out the martinet had handed over all her land and jewellery to her eviller daughter and shameless son-in-law, who never visited except for that one time when they arrived with stale murukkus and a lawyer in tow, bearing truckloads of deeds and documents for the old fool to sign. She could do nothing about it except fight the temptation to burn the shoebox with the lot of them in it and run away to the Himalayas and live among those naked yogis in the bracing cold.

The dastardly dame did not think it was a good idea for her to accept the teaching job offered to her by her stupid school. Whatever would people say if she actually worked for a living like some grubby peasant? So, she had tried to make it as a writer and failed spectacularly. Not that she had expected anything else. It was only in her dreams that she ever managed to succeed. Life had always been a less than stirring litany of abject failure. Some of her stories and articles were published in modest to respectable publications for embarrassingly measly sums and sometimes just for 'the honour of being published', but there was no steady work for her.

She would have probably made more as a hooker in the red-light districts. But she looked even more hideous with her clothes off and doubted her sojourn as a whore would be any more successful than her writing career. Although it was worth considering, if only to piss off her old-fashioned, ridiculously moralistic grandmother who nevertheless took the time to leer at her manservant and insist he massage her neck and feet every single day, moaning and groaning like a porn star as he ran his grubby paws over her.

Eventually, she did land a soul-sapping gig with an entertainment website. Now her job was to stalk celebs on social media and write gossipy or clickbait crap about them for a pittance. It was the best she could do, and so she looked at pics of the glitterati living it up in exotic locales, wrote about their affairs, boob jobs, drug habits, adorable kids, diet secrets, fitness regimes, current projects and wished all the while that she were dead. Death by envy, frustration and bitterness. A suitably wretched ending to an existence shorn of all things worth having. Or maybe a rape and robbery gone wrong, ending in her murder, would be a better way to go.

In a bid to distract herself from thoughts of dying, she had taken a stab at writing the great Indian novel. The ideas were there but for the life of her she couldn't find the fracking words to express them with anything close to literary merit. She recalled that the likes of Jeffrey Archer, Stephen King and Danielle Steel wrote compulsively for a few hours every day and she was determined to follow in their footsteps even if it killed her.

She made the time to write when she was not taking care of the old curmudgeon who had rescued her from the frying pan only to toss her into the fire, or trawling through social media to see what the celebs were up to, sometimes staying up all night to pound away at her laptop, praying it would churn out gold. Or silver. Or something. Or anything at all but the endless nothings.

There were glorious days when she managed as many as twenty pages of pure, unadulterated brilliance. But when she re-read the damn thing, it was always the same. Bilge. Garbage. Utter drivel. Sewage. It was true. The entire thing was worthless. So, there was nothing to do but to delete everything. And start over. Over and over. Till she got it right. If she got it right. Ever. Then she would agonize over why she had nothing to show for all that effort. So much wasted effort. It was her fate. A slow death by the endless expenditure of exhausting, unrewarding effort.

She didn't think she was properly suicidal. It was true that on some days she did go to sleep thinking it would be a blessing if she didn't wake up in the morning. But the funny thing was she thought a lot about dying without ever getting off her fat butt to do anything about it. Not surprisingly, like everything else in her life, her suicidal tendencies had the dubious distinction of being half-arsed. She probably ought to see a shrink, but nobody believed in shrinks in her neck of the woods, including herself. Crazy grandma, who could have probably used a shrink herself, believed there was nothing a visit to the temple and a dose of castor oil couldn't fix. Even bad genes inherited from an ill-omened daughter-in-law. So, they visited one too many temples, and she tried to shit away her overall dissatisfaction.

It was all very hopeless. But she continued to muck her way through a life she didn't want. Sans the dreams that had made it worth a damn. She forced herself to crawl out of bed every day, remembering the brilliant pages she had written the previous night and so heedlessly deleted, promising herself that she would never again delete a single word she wrote, even if it was utterly worthless, knowing that she would not, could not keep her word to herself.

Then she would shrug aside the self-loathing with difficulty and get cracking with her dull routine, which included making coffee and breakfast, lunch, dinner for the old lady and herself in addition to dusting, sweeping and swabbing. Her Evilness had always been parsimonious and did not believe in hiring maids or cooks, especially since her granddaughter could be counted on to take care of cleaning and maintenance with a little help from the manservant who had the unique gift for making a place dirtier as he pretended to clean it. Before the crone fell in the loo and dislocated her shoulder and smashed her hip bone, she had lorded over the kitchen and produced many a delicious if fattening meal, but now that her withered body was on the verge of quitting, urged otherwise by a will of steel, it fell to her to take care of meals as well.

So, she cooked, cleaned, wrote her abominable articles on the glam brigade, worked on her book, deleted her efforts almost as soon as they were laboriously expended, and saw the rest of her life play out in this unchanging spool of utter meaninglessness. And it would have gone down that way too if she had not been hunched over her laptop on that bitter night, groping for the words she would eventually erase with the brutal click of a key. She wished the damn flu would ease up so she could slip into the always troubled slumber from which she hoped never to wake up.

It was while rubbing her eyes in weary frustration that she espied the real witch, complete with a warty, hooked nose, unkempt hair, cracked fingernails and shapeless garments, helping herself to some food from the fridge. The foul fiend had even got her claws on the chocolate caramel brownies she had intended to devour later to feel better about the state of her writing.

She did not have the energy to scream in horror like those big-breasted women with disproportionately tiny waists in scary films as she watched the wicked witch chow down. Her head was throbbing from the depredations of the hostile viral takeover and was not up to dealing with any ramifications, if delusions and hallucinations were the latest symptoms of the life-threatening illness she was most certainly dealing with.

She sneezed into a tissue, examined the contents with mounting irritation and hardened her resolve to do absolutely nothing to save herself even if it meant being dragged down to the fires of hell and getting sodomized with a pitchfork. The part of her that wanted to somehow survive hoped that whatever it was would fade away into the shadow realm even as she turned back to her unforgiving screen and searched blindly in the hollow pit of nothingness for the words that would not come.

The witch cackled. It was such a cliché, but she jumped, hoping that the creature would settle for her grandmother's soul, sucking it out of her desiccated husk of a body after it had been drained of the blood and fluids that were surely past the expiry date, and leave her alone. Perhaps she should try her hand at horror.

Perhaps you should, the witch said. She cackled again.

Why are you here? I doubt you are here to grant three wishes, she whined, not bothering to ask how the witch knew what she had been thinking. What if she was granted three wishes? She would ask for success, fame and romance, she decided. If those choices weren't safe as shit, she didn't know what was.

Mercifully, the witch did not cackle again, for the damn creature was engaged in licking her talons clean. *I am not a lumbering genie in a lamp, in case you are confused*, the abomination sneered. *But I can give you everything that pathetic little heart of yours has ever wanted, in return for something that you would gladly part with.*

Everything?

Almost everything. The witch smirked. *At the end of our little transaction, you will have a completed manuscript, which will be a bestseller and later your precious script will be made into a movie, the culmination of a record-breaking deal if you play your cards right. Hell, you will even recover from the ailments that plague your mind and body, spared from the infernal angst and melodramatic agony that has been your lot in life. In return, all I ask is that you give me the only thing you don't want. Your worthless old grandmother who already has one foot in the grave.*

She was surprised when she hesitated. It sounded too good to be true and, therefore, it was almost certainly too good to be true. Wasn't it? But what did she have to lose? And the witch was right. Her grandmother was at death's door even though she insisted on clinging to life with her gnarly old hands. Still, she paused.

I haven't got all night! What will it be? Your dreams in exchange for your grandmother, who is already as good as dead, or not? The witch began to fade like an amateurish CGI job.

Wait! She said quickly. *I will find the words to finish my novel, won't I? My book will go on to be a massive bestseller and a gargantuan blockbuster?* (She wondered if she should insist that her book win critical acclaim as well and a slew of prestigious as frack awards.) *You can guarantee that?*

She was glad that the dreams were back. Though it sucked that she had the worst of colds even in that state of sublime fantasy that had formerly been sacrosanct, free from interlopers who wanted to damn her forever.

Of course! The witch rolled her grotesque eyes. *I give you a personal guarantee, though you will do well to remember that nobody can predict the future. Not even the countless gods out there. But with my help, you, who has always had nothing, will finally have everything you have ever wanted. If you are willing to get off that well-fed backside of yours and do the needful that is.*

She recoiled. Was this monstrosity expecting her to snuff the life out of old flatulence with a pillow or something? Or maybe poison her? Or stick a knife in her heart? Was she supposed to get her hands dirty?

The demon spawn laughed out loud. *You don't have to do anything of the sort.* The creature looked at her appraisingly. *All you have to do is agree to trade her life, which is almost at an end, in exchange for the fulfilment of your desires. Just say the word and we will have a deal.*

She did not hesitate this time. *I will do it. You can have HER.* She flinched inwardly. Deals made under duress when you were experiencing what was clearly a fever dream did not count, did they?

Wise decision! The witch cackled one last time. *And it does count.*

The dispenser of desires disappeared in a puff of green smoke. Of all the clichés, this one was the worst!

She wrote thirty pages that night. And they were good. Even better, she did not feel the irresistible urge to delete them all before she fell asleep. Because they were genuinely good. For the first time in forever, she fell asleep with the merest hint of a smile on her lips.

When she came to, it was not in her own bed, but the one in the guest bedroom downstairs. Grandmother's family doctor was long gone but his handsome son ministered to her needs now and he was talking to the old she-devil. She was looking better than ever and leering lasciviously at Doc Handsome, who was assuring her that her granddaughter would live now that she had been fed intravenously and the fever had broken. She felt the needle in her vein and resisted the urge to pull it out and stick it in her eye.

Of course it had been a fever dream! Too bad the crushing disappointment on seeing the old hag hale and hearty would not kill her. Doc Handsome was telling the bitch that if she came for weekly check-ups as per usual, there was no reason she wouldn't live forever now that her hip and shoulder had mended perfectly. She did not doubt him and sighed aloud.

Doc Handsome heard her. *You gave us all a scare*, he scolded her gently. The kindness in his eyes made her want to bawl. He was always nice and made her feel like a real person and not the sack of shit she always saw in the mirror. At that moment she loved him with all her heart and would have gladly become his whore if he wished to cheat on his wife. *You really shouldn't self-medicate*, he told her mock severely. He handed her a bar of white Toblerone and winked at her.

She was touched he remembered her mentioning that it was her favourite. Most folks would have nodded and glanced meaningfully at her corpulent form but not Doc Handsome. He told her he had a weakness for the stuff too. She tried to croak her thanks, but he merely shook her hand, smiled his kind smile and was gone, with her stupid ass grandmother in tow.

To her surprise she made a speedy recovery. To her relief (and only mild disappointment), Grandmother dearest was in fine fettle too, spinning like a dervish, cooking and baking up a storm. She had more time to write and, to her surprise, the words did not elude her. Thirty pages became 380 as she worked with a joyful abandon that was the best of boons. She was so busy writing, she forgot to hate herself and fill the aching emptiness inside with all the food she could eat.

The months rolled by in a haze of profound euphoria as the floodwaters of her creativity spilled forth in a merry rush. And she wrote and wrote and wrote. Who needed fricking witches and their contracts that demanded signatures of blood? Not her, that was for sure. All she had needed was confidence. When she finally typed the last word of her manuscript, she thought her heart would explode with happiness. In fact, she was so glad, it was almost possible to ignore the unease that was lurking just by the periphery of conscious thought and bounded rationality. Besides, her wonderful grandmother was looking positively robust.

As for herself, she looked and felt great. For once, stalking celebs paid off and she got the name of a superstar's literary agent. She emailed the guy, following the submission guidelines down to the very last letter. Ordinarily, she would have died of anxiety, but she was now on the top of the world, and she knew no fear. Of course, he replied and said that it was *wunderbar*. He was confident she would get a decent advance. And she did. More than fairly decent. Her happiness was now complete. It was even more complete when the big studios expressed more than a passing interest in her manuscript and began a bidding war for the rights.

There was more. The old dear had been working

on finding a match for her with a vengeance and soon her efforts paid off and she was engaged to a software dude (what exactly did those chaps do anyway?) based in Singapore. He was bald (in the manner of Jason Statham) and charming as hell. Not only did he buy her one of those ridiculously expensive Android phones, but he also patiently taught her how to use it. If that were not enough, he sent her flowers, chocolates, perfumes, soft toys, Anokhi kurtas (anarkalis that flattered her form) and sparkly thingies in classy gift-wrapped boxes. He flew down every once in a while to take her out to lunch and make out with her in his car (a silver Audi he had rented).

He was proud he was marrying an author and was almost as excited as she was since the book was scheduled for a summer release, just after their honeymoon (they were going to Europe for three glorious weeks!). It was all too magical for words. Her beloved grandmother, famed for her parsimony, showed her the trousseau she had put together for her wedding. It was a queen's ransom. There were silk saris, silverware enough to fill a truck and so many diamonds it was indecent. This was in addition to the prime property the wonderful soul had bequeathed to her and an apartment in the city, which was being rented out at present. She was officially rich now!

It was all too perfect for words. So perfect that it was

easy to brush aside the stray tendrils of rising dread. What happened in feverish dreams did not count, she assured herself. And witches were merely a figment torn loose from nightmares – the way fairy godmothers did not exist outside of fairy tales. She devoured a second helping of roast chicken placed before her by the old sweetheart, who smiled encouragingly and said that a healthy appetite produced healthy babies.

She swallowed and said nothing. They went for grandmother's hospital visit together. It was reassuring to note that the grand dame did not need the assistance of a cane. Dressed in her finest silks and dripping with diamonds, she might as well have been visiting the queen rather than her doctor.

Doc Handsome was waiting at the entrance, waving cheerily at them. He didn't have to, of course, but it was just like him. They were inside when grandmother pulled her aside. *I am getting forgetful, dear, will you run down to the car and bring back that gift box of assorted nuts and treats? It is the very least I can do for this nice boy who has restored me to full health. A good boy! Just like his father before him.*

She didn't have to be told twice. There was a skip in her step as she made her way down the winding path to the parking lot. It was best to hurry if she wished to make it to the car before the chauffeur took off on one of his ridiculously lengthy tea breaks.

She felt the explosion before she heard it. When she turned back, the hospital was still standing but it had lost entire chunks of itself. She took in the gaping holes, billowing smoke, flying bits of concrete, sudden sparks, ear-splitting shrieks and the distant wail of a clanging alarm, praying that it was a nightmare that would dissipate the second she woke up.

In a daze she ran towards the scorching inferno. Her grandmother was afraid of dying alone. She needed to be there for her. It was the very least she could do. Someone tried to hold her back with a surprisingly fierce grip, cracked soot-stained fingernails digging painfully into her flesh. Prising herself free and shoving the do-gooder aside with violence borne of her terror and guilt, she was running full tilt towards the remains of the hospital when the second blast tore through the barely standing hospital, obliterating it and all in the immediate vicinity entirely.

The witch did not cackle. It was such a pity after all. But these things happen, the termagant mused to herself as she cast one last withering look at the scene of utter ruin and devastation before vanishing from the scene.

Irenosen Okojie is a Nigerian British author whose work pushes the boundaries of form, language and ideas. Her novel, *Butterfly Fish*, and short story collections, *Speak Gigantular* and *Nudibranch*, have won and been nominated for multiple awards. Her journalism has been featured in *New York Times*, *Observer*, the *Guardian* and *Huffington Post*. She was a contributing editor for *The White Review*. She co-presented the BBC's *Turn Up for the Books* podcast, alongside Simon Savidge and Bastille frontman Dan Smith. Her work has been optioned for the screen. She has also judged various literary prizes, including the Dylan Thomas Prize, the Gordon Burn Prize and the BBC National Short Story Award. She was a judge for the 2023 Women's Prize for Fiction. Vice chair of the Royal Society of Literature, she was awarded an MBE 'for services to literature' in 2021. In 2023, she was named a visionary artist in *Red* magazine's 'The next 25 visionaries to watch' list. She is the director and founder of Black to the Future festival, a multidisciplinary Afrofuturist festival.

Photograph of Irenosen Okojie by David Kwaw Mensah

Enacting revenge, she says, is justified retribution. It's taking back what was stolen, making space for powerful transformations of what was lost.

7

Following

IRENOSEN OKOJIE

I PLUCKED YOU from the garden like a root vegetable. A tiny man, you still had soil in the creases of your skin after I dusted you off on the oak kitchen table.

You pointed at me. We studied each other as if we were foreign objects. You spoke in a low, guttural language I didn't understand. Your arms waved at the light breaking in my eyes. I stared at the slit in your miniature penis, growing it with my mouth. The garden door groaned; a torn, white plastic bag blew in. I remembered the fortune teller then. I remembered paying for a flower that died on the way back and being handed white seeds after a loaded smile. That night, I'd slipped one seed beneath my tongue and planted the rest, only for things to grow in sleep.

That was three months ago.

Now, you jumped up and down on the table, baring jagged teeth, curling your hands into fists. I hunched down, held a finger to my lips. 'Quiet!' I ordered. 'Or I'll put you in the freezer for a few hours.' You stopped then, understanding my tone perfectly. You smelled of soil and dampness, of things born. I pressed my lips to your face, wanting to swallow you whole.

'Bath time,' I said, pleasant, almost chirpy. I rummaged through the kitchen cabinets, the sound of implosions playing in my head. I filled a deep, plastic bowl with warm water and soaped you down as you wriggled reluctantly.

'Be still,' I instructed. Slick from soapy water, you dodged my grasp, settling into sly limbs. Outside, a large vehicle came to a halt, churning. A rubbish truck probably.

'Bitch! Bitch! Bitch!' you hurled, suddenly speaking English. The words were a rope dangling between my organs. I grabbed you and dumped you in the cutlery drawer, slamming it shut. The clatter of utensils followed me to the sitting room where the widescreen TV waited.

I flicked it on. Images of you rolling between knives and forks interrupted programmes.

Later, I fished you out. You were bloody and smiling.

'Haha haha. Set me on fire, find the matches.' Your grizzly smile stretched, threatening to leave your face. I carried you upstairs, wiped your cuts with cotton wool, watching them become blood clouds in my hands.

At night I plied you with vodka. It was funny to see you stumble around drunk, beneath the cruel glow of flickering candlelight. When you collapsed, I pressed my ear to your chest, comforted by the sound of heavy panting.

I bought a yellow hamster wheel that squeaked. It sat by the crack on the white window ledge in the bedroom. My eyes returned to it repeatedly, as though it was a small piece of thunder waiting to snag the wheel. Running on that wheel kept you busy and resentful, a tiny fist under the world's crinkly curtain. The sound of turns haunted the rooms. I heard it while drying dishes and polishing cabinets downstairs that housed pictures faced down. It bounced off the thin, silver hands of my leather watch. At times I saw you rushing towards me, waving your fists and talking in another language I couldn't understand. And the wheel had replaced your right leg, squeaking loudly, punctuating the sentences of an unfamiliar language.

On the second day, I served you a portion of pasta coated in a wild mushroom and leek sauce.

'Please eat,' I said, pushing the saucer of steaming food towards you. Five minutes earlier, you'd torn clumps of matted hair from your head. It lay next to the food as though part of a twisted menu. You took a teaspoon full. I watched your lean, changeable face for approval.

'This isn't very good. I wish you'd disappear.' You scrunched your features up. The words formed a stone map in my gut. Later that evening, you ran on the yellow wheel till it became snippets of a life spinning beneath your feet. The night was a canvas studded with stars, morphing from one day to the next. In its sky, we made love on a knife's edge, blinded by the blood from our cuts. Afterwards, a two-headed animal shedding skin in the broken ceiling dangled down.

We sat in my white bathtub under a sea. Above, a man wearing tattered black trousers played the piano, Beethoven's *Symphony No. 9*, to us taking our clothes off. Clothes that became fish in the grip of ripples, a minute or so later a polka-dot fish swam past.

'Sorry, sorry, sorry,' you muttered at me as though it was a mantra.

'Why are you telling me this here?' I asked, a naked woman next to a little naked man.

'It's so blue!' You laughed. 'Like waking up having a different lens and because things lose their definition here.'

Just then a gold packet of Marlboro Lights floated. We took deep breaths, tasting cigarettes on our tongues.

'Well, it's shitty! It's shitty of you to say my pasta

wasn't good.' I pointed my finger accusingly. It felt like slow motion.

'I didn't say you were a bad person. I said your pasta was average. Sorry you cooked a crappy meal. Sorry, sorry. Sorry.' Mouth over my belly button, you pulled three threads. The piano man played frenetically. I sensed urgency in his strokes. His reflection was a shimmering looking glass. Your mouth curled over my nipples, sucked gently. The sweet sensation felt like falling into a trap. The bathtub spun away. Fish made from cotton and polyester wrestled things down into the bed of the sea. Only I couldn't see what they were, distracted by tiny tremors of pleasure spreading over my body. The coolness of the water made me semi-alert. Then I saw that the fish were wrestling memories. Images of me laughing on a bridge, dancing in the supermarket aisle, buying a lamp with the half-lizard woman emblazoned on the shade. In each one, the grip of someone holding my hand just outside the frame loosened.

'I brought you here because...' You left the sentence hanging, strung up on the three threads that tugged it away.

'Why are we having this conversation here?'

We came up for air, back in the tub with cold water sloshing down the sides. Our clothes stuck to dimpled bodies. A wooden afro comb had fallen in and was unpicking a tide. I held you in my hands as you tried to scramble off. You were speaking Japanese. And I could have sworn you did that on purpose.

In bed I tossed and turned. I worried about all your possible routes of escape; through a watermark in the bathroom ceiling, hiding in a beer bottle I'd accidentally thrown away, disappearing into a pause from a conversation outside.

The following morning, you began to speak in tongues at breakfast. Crumbs of toast spilled on the table as you talked. You spoke in tongues running up my thighs, eyeing the front door from the thinly carpeted staircase, as if you wanted to squeeze your limbs through the keyhole. You watched my face. I waited for you to walk into my iris and become a tiny silhouette trapped there.

I stuck needles in your skin to silence the noise inside my head. I made you become a doll. When bulbs of blood appeared, I used them to colour the sea beneath a ship I'd drawn.

Days passed, a week became a fortnight and then a month. Our dysfunctional routines continued. I blindfolded you and rammed cockroaches down your throat. Tied you inside bags of rotten fish and listened while you vomited. I stuffed small things inside my privates, forcing you to find them as I stroked my collarbone. We went out on day trips. You stayed in my pocket on rumbling trains. The feeling of you burrowing reassured me. You tried to grow other heads in there, between the seams and warm lining. I put a stop to that, squeezing them until they disappeared. On one outing to the Science Museum, you spoke in Swahili. I had become used to these random bursts of language and travelling by tongue.

A bank-holiday Monday arrived, bright and breezy. In the morning, I found you beside my wardrobe, clutching the leg of a pair of navy men's trousers; tears ran down your cheeks. I was throwing the bins away when you rushed through the half-open front door. Horrified, I watched you duck beneath the small arched gate, past a smattering of cars lining the street and over to the other side. The bins dropped with a thud. My heartbeat quickened. The purple, flannel dressing gown I wore came undone. I was barefoot but there was no time. No time to run back in and grab shoes. I scrambled after you. The warm concrete was hard and unforgiving beneath my feet. You were surprisingly quick. I could just about spot your tiny figure in an ill-fitting tracksuit I'd made, darting into a side path towards the main road. My mouth felt dry and grainy, as though coated in sand. I ignored the puzzled glances of passersby. I was too busy trying to breathe, to produce a survivor's stroke for an indoor sea that had slipped outside. The smell of carpet pine clung to my nostrils. I stepped on a flattened can of ginger beer acting as a fleeting shoe. Then we were both in the wide, slanting road, wild-haired and wild-eyed. I dived to grab you, into the sounds of tires screeching and engines humming like bees. Car horns screamed. The sting from falling on my knees was sharp. I lost my breath to the gaps between the trees. And a big red bus was flying. No. 58. The driver had a white shirt on. All I could think as you struggled in my hands was *the driver is wearing a sky.*

Indoors, inside the kitchen, we trembled. I held you beneath a chair leg, hovered it close to your Adam's apple. Then grabbed a fork and stabbed it into your thigh.

'Aargh! Please, stop,' you yelped, speaking English again. The piano man played in the distance, on a spiralling, silver staircase. His clothes began to come off, until he was naked. Piano keys uprooted like large teeth as the melancholy tune became more and more haphazard. I started to cry then because heartbreak smelled like half-eaten rum cake at a breakfast table. I remembered that morning always, you see? The morning that you went out for a packet of gold Marlboro Lights and never came back. I remembered the agonising waiting, knocking our wedding photos face down on shelves months after and wailing in the musty wardrobe between your clothes. I turned over my sacrifices as if they were coins. Bits of myself I'd lost in gloves, doorway cracks and printer ink heads. How I'd travelled through echoes, silences, curved fingers over piano keys.

All the routes home I'd built for you in the static.

'I'm sorry! *Pardonnez-moi*! *Kite m'esplike*!' you pleaded, mixing languages as your bottom half began crumbling into bloody soil.

I told you I'd chased your laughter through tunnels and pathways. That I'd been following. And holding the chair leg pressed against your throat, I whispered all the things I'd done to resurrect you.

Author, TEDx speaker, columnist and mentor, **Kiran Manral** has been a journalist, researcher, festival curator and entrepreneur in previous avatars. She has published books across genres in fiction and non-fiction. She has received multiple awards, such as the Women Achievers Award by Young Environmentalists Association, the International Women's Day Award 2018 from the Indian Council for UN Relations supported by the Ministry of Women and Child Welfare, Government of India, for excellence in the field of writing and the Womennovator 1000 Women of Asia Award 2021. In 2022, she was named amongst the 75 Iconic Indian women in STEAM by Red Dot Foundation and Beyond Black, in collaboration with the Office of the Principal Scientific Advisor, Government of India, and British High Commission, New Delhi.

She believes that revenge is best served piping hot, with sparklers around the dish and flambéed at the table.

8

The Night of the Supermoon

KIRAN MANRAL

IT WAS THE perfect night for this kind of a thing. By this kind of a thing, I mean the supernatural. The supernatural occurs, most people believe, on nights when the moon is hidden, the sky is dark, and unearthly creatures roam the surface of the Earth. Most nights aren't perfect, but we haunt nonetheless. It is what we're meant to do, to haunt. To roam the surface of the Earth, wanton with the desire for revenge; it is what feeds us, what makes us stronger, what keeps us here tethered to this dimension.

Rubbish. We just are. As living people are. Confused and here not of our own volition, wondering if this is it, to be condemned to an eternity in the same set of clothes, with not a chance of a good meal or a hot bath.

It is quite the microcosm of the afterworld here. There is a crematorium right behind, next door to the church, and a monastery at the back of the wall of the ruins I inhabit, and that quite adds to the numbers of those already deceased but not quite gone. I don't really keep pace with what the other creatures that inhabit these ruins do. There are ghosts, ghouls, a couple of the undead who keep slithering out of their graves when they need feeding, the occasional demon who arrives to carry off a sulking soul who has managed to extend their stay here, citing the need for revenge, although what revenge they can carry out by being stuck here in the cemetery next to the ruins no one knows.

Most folks avoid this place after dark. No one who ever stayed back here through the night has gone back with their wits intact. One would think that by now folks would have wised up and realized that it was a bad idea to be here when the protective rays of the sun have sunk beneath the horizon. But a couple of times a year, one gets the odd specimen, a young man staying back in the ruins for the night, on a dare. A desolate young bride, hiding here from the torture she faced back in her marital home, the company of spirits preferable to the humans she has had to live with. Even us ghosts have a code of honour – we let her be in her misery, keep the viler of us away from her. You could say we protect her, even though she has no clue of the wars that are unfurling around her.

At the witching hour, one of us will softly seed hope in her mind. Whoever said that ghosts are vicious and vengeful? We are the same as we were when alive, some of us gentle and quiet, and the others making a complete nuisance of themselves.

Back to this night. Perfect for hauntings, as I mentioned earlier. I often regret having passed into the afterlife wearing this pair of jeans and this sweatshirt with the big pink heart on the front. It doesn't really make for a great ghost outfit. Therefore, let me take this opportunity to warn you good folks who might be reading this. Always dress well. What you wear when you die will be your ghost outfit for eternity. It is really difficult to haunt unwary humans when I appear in front of them, shimmering in skinny jeans and a sweatshirt with a happy pink heart bursting out of it; they think me to be a lost college student, and offer me their water and snacks. None of them think for a moment that skinny fits have been out of fashion for a long, long while. And if there is anything that really distresses me even in this non-corporeal state, it is the fact that I am out of date with the fashion of the times, now that trousers and denims are loose enough for four limbs to fit comfortably into one leg and still have space left.

But where are my manners, dear reader. I am, as you might have guessed, a ghost. A deceased one. A dead soul. A lingering soul. Why I am lingering about here, in these ruins, I still do not know. When I was alive, I was rather the looker, I'm told, although I could have done with a few inches in the height department and a nose that was a little perter, while we're at it.

Anyway, tonight was the first full moon after the autumnal equinox. For another, it was a supermoon. A big one. Also, a blue moon. Full moons were good for business. Supermoons were even better. The moon, a big roundel of yellow cheddar cheese, hung in the sky, undecided, and rather low. It would climb higher, I knew. It always did, and then it plopped back down over the horizon and returned the next evening, a tad diminished for the journey.

Supermoons meant students, amateur astronomers and the curious out on this hillside, facing the ruins in a bid to capture the most fascinating photographs of the phenomenon against the ruins. Or, if I were to put it more appropriately, silhouetted against what was now my permanent home, given I'd lost my chance when they'd urged me to go towards the light. You see, I was still looking back, expecting them to tell me they'd made a mistake. But, well, obviously they hadn't, and I was quite dead. Or at least my body was. A bad fall from the high walls – so dangerous to take selfies on the parapets. And it was a new iPhone too. Accidental death. No post-mortem. Some crying, mainly from my parents, and a couple of friends, and that was that. The end of me. They say you die twice, once when your physical body dies, and then when your name is taken for the last time. I still had to have my second death. It would be a while, I guessed. My parents were still alive, the pandit came home for the shrāddh puja. My photographs were still all over the house. I would probably die again, and for the final time, after both my parents died. After all, who else would think about me, remember me, miss me? I didn't even miss myself.

I laughed; it felt like the moon laughed back at me. Monstrously huge it was today. The seas and oceans would be surging towards it, the blood in human veins would be drawn to it, to the pull of this rock in a vacuum 3,84,400 kilometres away, the fifth largest moon in our planetary system, locked into orbit around the Earth in a strange covenant, while weirdly enough, moderating the wobble in our axis, making the climate stable enough, creating tides that pushed and pulled the waters on the surface of the planet in a rhythm that has guided seafarers and fishermen for millennia. For centuries we thought there was only one moon, until Galileo Galilei spotted the four moons of Jupiter and got bunged into house arrest for all his trouble, of course, it was also the fact that he went about declaring that the Earth revolved around the sun, and you don't go around saying things like that when the church basically believes in the opposite thing... but there you are, and here we are.

The moon, born of a collision most likely with a Mars-sized body, is by itself without atmosphere, without life, without anything that would make it attractive like a good mall or a decent pub, yet countries flock there by the dozens, putting up their flags, trying to claim bits and pieces of territory.

A supermoon meant that fools wandered into the ruins trying to make out, get high behind the crumbling walls or fulfil dares by staying through the night when all had left, and one could entertain oneself by giving them a bit of scare if one chose to. That bored me now though – one scared person is much the same as the other and the novelty had palled after the first few times.

I was at my usual perch, on the wall holding up the broken-down gate, looking at the crowds passing the old ruins within. Groups of students, a few families, a school group escorted by enthusiastic teachers, setting up their dinky little telescopes. All fighting for a good spot right on top of the grassy knolls behind the ruins. She caught my eye, she did, holding onto the hand of her little boy like it was a matter of life or death. Dressed in a pair of loose linen trousers, an oversized shirt, a sling bag across her torso, her hair cropped to a short bob at her chin, her eyes huge in a face that was all angles and planes, like a doe's. She was beautiful. The man with her, her husband I assumed, sent a shiver down my spine. When you die, you become extra perceptive to the good and evil in living humans. The man was ruthless and cruel and had been here before. I could sense that by the sureness with which he walked to a bit of the knoll, shaded by a tree and bushes. She was unsure, hesitant. She followed. There was a turmoil in her I could sense, but I couldn't step beyond the gate of the ruins to suss out what it was. There is a boundary, you know, beyond which we cannot leave if we are psychically bound to a place. If our psychic boundary is a person, well, heaven help that person because we'll go wherever that person goes. They really can't escape us, no more than we can escape them.

Next door, at the cemetery, it was business as usual. A fresh body had been buried just a couple of days ago, and the owner was flitting around, trying to strike up conversation and be neighbourly with the other dead souls and the undead crawling out of their graves, waiting for an unwary human to enter the premises.

A gang of young boys, beer cans in their hands, came into the compound, swinging the gate wide open, kicking a stone or two, one taking a piss on the walls. They couldn't have been more than 22, 23 at the very most. They were a hardened lot, toughened by life and circumstances already. Their faces were planed from a childhood of hunger and deprivation, their hands nifty from their tricks for survival.

The ghouls had already sniffed them out and were moving swiftly to this side of the ruins, circling them intently, preparing for their attack. *Phasma philinnion*, a category of cacodemons, I had learnt in my time spent here. Also known as *ghulan, jikiniki, aswang* in various parts of the world. They could not harm me, my body had been taken away for post-mortem and cremation, but they'd already been through the contents of the graves in the cemetery and were always on the lookout for fresh human flesh and blood. We would not intervene. That was the way of the world, predators preyed, the carrion feeders fed, other animals watched.

The screams would come, I knew, after some hours had passed, the beers had been downed, and whatever they'd brought to smoke up or inject into their bloodstreams had been smoked up and injected. Ghouls were patient like that, they waited respectfully until the night was deep and the moon was high, and silence resounded through the stone passages like the echo of a heart thumping in fear.

The family I'd been watching sat down on the grass, observing the moon. The mother quickly set up a telescope she must have been carrying in the bag swinging from her hand. I kept watching them, strangely drawn to them. It must have been close to midnight. After a while, the mother got up from the ground and looked around, her movements strange, disjointed. Perhaps she was not used to sitting on the ground, it could lock your knees. She turned towards the ruins and began walking purposefully towards us. The general populace of the ruins – spirits, ghosts, spectres, ghouls, shades, wraiths, phantoms, call us what you may – watched on, curious and perplexed. It was uncharacteristic for a young woman to enter these premises. Apart from the otherworldly residents, even the very human creatures who entered this place after sun-fall were not the safest to be around. I swooped down towards her out of curiosity, and an odd sense of protectiveness. She shivered as I hovered next to her but kept on walking to the ruins with a determination that seemed worrisome. The father and child were engrossed in watching the moon through the little dinky telescope and didn't seem to have noticed that she had stepped away.

Where was she going? Did she not realize this was no place to enter? This was an accursed site, and whoever entered went away twisted and scarred permanently by the curse that had befallen the place. It seeped into them, through some strange osmosis, percolating deep into their subconscious, through the air perhaps, through the pain of all those who had died here, the monks and those they had never allowed to leave here alive or with their sanity intact. Some lost their mind from the howling that sawed into their brains, an unearthly howling, cries for help that no one beyond these walls could hear, a howling that began some nights at exactly the time the fire had engulfed these walls.

Perhaps she was going to relieve herself behind a wall, as there were no public toilets here in this place. The municipal authorities had never deemed them necessary even though there was a steady trickle of tourists here most days to visit the magnificence of the ruined tower. It was a sight worth seeing, I must admit, even though being stuck here for the past so many years had kind of ruined its charm for me. We were on holy ground, or what was once holy ground. A church established by a monastic order, with living quarters for the monks attached to the church. Impressive when it was built, it had survived invasions, and attacks and plagues and floods and famines, only to be struck down by lightning and fire so only the belfry remained blackened and crumbling, the huge iron bell within still holding on through the ages and some walls. The monks had abandoned the premises rather than rebuild it, considering it cursed. The wrath of the Lord had struck it down. There were abominations going on within those walls, the whispers went. The evil had perished in fire, their shades remained, bound by our ethers to this place. There were horrors that had occurred within those walls that even the monks would not speak of. On some dark nights, the ground beneath the ruins growled and shook, and the bell tolled of its own accord. The authorities had put up a fence and a sign that warned people from entering and staying back after dark, but there was no watchman to enforce the sign.

The woman was walking rather briskly and entered the gates without a moment's hesitation. I sidled right beside her, trying to gauge her intentions. She didn't know of the horrors within, I guessed, for no one in their sane mind would come within the gates after night had fallen. She was pretty, I realized looking at her closely, a prettiness that was tempered with a gentle softness that made one want to protect her, to keep her safe from the creatures that were whooshing around, weighing whether she merited any attention or should be ignored. She walked with purpose right to the tower leading up to the belfry and began climbing the crumbling stairs, lit up by the light of the blazing moon. The moon smiled down at us all, a smile that was fangs dripping blood. It made us all jump out of our non-existent skins. I fluttered next to her, trying to get inside her head and suss out her thoughts. It was not such a good idea to climb up, I tried telling her, the steps were steep and the view was great but not worth risking one's life. After all, she had a child to think of. She sighed.

The ghouls looked up from where they had been circling the drunk revellers, waiting for the right moment to pounce, sniffing fresh blood untainted by alcohol. One reared up next to me, fetid and putrid, rank with the odour of decaying flesh. I recoiled unwittingly, a strangely human reaction, given I could barely smell or taste anything.

'Is she planning on jumping?' it asked conversationally. That would mean fresh meat without the trouble of actually killing her. It was a lazy sort, this one. It liked to wait until the others were done and then feast on the remains, rather than hunt prey. We'd chatted occasionally; it really meant no harm. It was just doing what it had been created to do, scavenge on carrion.

'Nice and fleshy in bits, rest all bone,' it said, looking at her breasts.

'Let her be,' I said. 'You have those boys down there for tonight. There should be enough for all of you.'

'She's going to jump anyway, it would be a shame to let it go waste, I mean, we are the vultures of the other world.' It laughed, a laugh that had I had my human ears, would have shredded my eardrums into strips of bleeding membrane.

'If she doesn't jump, you won't eat her, will you? Not while she's alive, right?'

'I prefer my meat dead and unlikely to be squirming and screaming. Yes, only after she jumps and dies.'

Perhaps, I told myself, I could persuade her not to jump. I'd already figured out how to ingress into the minds of the living and seed thoughts, it was easier when they were emotional and pre-occupied – they didn't realize I was in their heads until it was too late to try and push me out. I seeped into her mind through her ear. I was in a body again after a long, long while, and it felt good, heavy, real. It felt crowded though. We plodded on past the second flight of stairs leading to the top of the belfry, me and her. It was quite surreal how she calmly moved aside to let me take over, almost like she was expecting me. Gosh, I missed being anchored to the earth. This floating around was all nice and good, but a slight breeze could take you off miles from where you intended to go, and then being wrenched back to where one was rooted was very, very painful.

Here I was, looking through her eyes. I should make her stop moving upwards, I told myself, but it seemed like I was powerless against her will. She didn't intend to die. That I knew now. But I didn't know what it was that she had come up here to do.

I blinked her eyes. I could see the church as it had

been before it was burnt down. There were four towers then, I could see their ghostly outlines. The church was shimmering in front of me, slowly, like a hologram projection coming into focus. The monastery attached to the church also solidified before my eyes, or rather, my borrowed eyes. The monks were bustling about, at their chores, some at prayer, others closing the windows, shutting the doors, snuffing the candles out, winding up their tasks for the day. I blinked hard again. Surely, I was imagining this. These phantasmagorical images were not real, I told myself, they were imprints from the energy of the time this place was bustling and alive and filled with incense and prayer and chants. Somehow, I had been transported to that time, that place, I was living in that world. Somewhere above us, the bell began tolling on its own, long pealing chimes.

'What is happening?' I spoke aloud through her lips, her tongue, her voice. No one answered. I didn't expect anyone to.

Her legs were still moving upwards, I couldn't seem to stop them. I was being carried on up with her, right to the top where the ghostly bell was still tolling, a bell I could see now, with her eyes. We'd reached the top of the belfry. She stood, we stood, just beneath the bell. A monk was pulling the rope, frowning with the exertion, beads of sweat on his forehead. He shimmered, like a projection on a screen. I egressed out of her body and her mind. She stood breathing heavily on the edge of a stairway that was almost collapsing. The ghoul lingered a few steps beneath, waiting for her to jump. She stood there a long while, waiting, a soft smile playing on her face. Waiting for exactly what, I did not know.

'Don't jump,' I whispered into her mind.

Soft as a whisper the answer came, 'Don't worry, I won't.'

There was a commotion at the gate, her husband and son entered. She stood up, looking down at them, the light from the moon dancing full on her face, casting high shadows and sharp planes.

'Stupid woman,' he said in an aside, and then shouted loud, 'Don't jump. Wait.'

She waited calmly. He instructed the child to stand right there and not move. The child looked up, confused and perplexed, wondering what was happening. The woman waited for him to climb all the way, waiting like she had been waiting all these years for him to come to her, to realize that it was her that he wanted. The moon shone brightly above them all, above us all, pulsing through the clouds that floated past its surface, darkness, and then light bursting through, lighting up the crumbling stairs, deepening the shadows, pulling out the creatures of the shadows into its light, who gasped in fear when they saw the glory of its huge, radiant disc.

He reached the top and grabbed her. 'Are you mad?' he gasped. 'I'll have the police on my back if you die. Did you even think what it would do to my reputation, the headlines in the newspapers? The company stock?'

She smiled. It was the beautiful smile of someone who had absolutely no intention of dying and with a gesture so smooth it was almost invisible, she pushed him off the tower with a surreal force that her petite body seemed incapable of containing. His expression as he fell was first of astonishment and then horror as he realized what had happened. His scream faded before he hit the ground, her laughter echoed as his scream faded. He was quite dead, I think, before his body broke and crumpled on the stones below, just as mine had. The child screamed now, a primal scream of terror that pierced the skies and made the stones of the tower vibrate. The dead man's ghost rose up from his body, confused and looking around, as if trying to figure out what had just happened. The ghoul rushed down, eager to drag the body off into the ruins and begin devouring it before the others laid claim to it. The newly minted ghost stared around, confused, still reconciling himself to the fact that he was now, in fact, dead, and the body lying like a hunk of meat on the stones was his. The group of boys came running out from the corner they'd holed up in, on hearing the commotion.

'What happened to me?' he asked. I waited a bit to see if the white people or the grey people came for him. When no one did, I knew he was destined to be part of our lot confined to these ruins. 'And what are you doing here? I thought you were dead.'

'Well,' I replied. 'You're dead to begin with. Your wife pushed you down.' He looked down at himself, confused.

The woman rushed down, grabbed the child by the hand and rushed out of the gates without a second glance at the crumpled body of her husband lying there.

'Why did she do that? And why is that creature taking my body behind the wall?'

'Oh, ignore him, he'll just eat you up, and be done with it. It's better you don't watch. And anyway, it doesn't make a difference what happens to your body now, does it?'

He shook his head. He seemed to be taking this death business much better than I had when I died.

'So why did she do that?'

He shook his head. 'I have no clue. Stupid woman,' he said again. 'I was on the verge of closing a huge deal too.'

But I needed to know. I flitted back to her; she had almost passed through the gate; once she had passed through, I would have no power over her. I ingressed into her mind again, stopping her body where it was, mid-stride. There was only darkness within and a sense of multiple presences. I ingressed further, sifting through memories, thoughts, deep dark tunnels of consciousness, sifting and pulling, until I reached the deepest recesses of the mind where I found hiding, in a dark, enclosed space, a fractal of the conscious mind, the soul of the actual person who owned the body. She was lovely, as lovely as her body was. I reached out to her, took her hand. The body shuddered and convulsed in agony. This woman, the owner of the body, was terrified, and struggled to free herself from my grasp.

'Help me,' she whispered.

'I don't understand.'

'She'll kill you too,' she said, trying to fold herself back into the tiny, enclosed space she had been hiding in.

'Who will?' I replied, confused.

Another presence blasted through, barrelling me away from her, out of her. 'You're already dead. Get out of this body now.'

I felt a force push me out of the body. Physically throw me out. I grabbed hard. It was substance I could grab, the ether of another discorporate being like me. We fell out of the body, both of us. The body we'd both vacated sagged to the ground like the air had been let out of her. The child holding onto the hand of the woman who was on the ground began sobbing. She sat up and cradled him, also sobbing, then lifted him to his feet and ran out of the gate, dragging him behind her.

I was holding hard onto another ghost. She was no ordinary garden variety ghost like me, but a spirit consumed by vengeance, pale of skin and red of eye, with hair streaming down her back, long and serpentine curls that had a life of their own, moving, writhing, a thousand snakes confined by tails attached to her scalp. I was looking at a chudail. She was young, a beauty, full lips and doe eyes, the dusky skin of violent sunsets, and her smile was the glint of a thousand serrated knives sharpened on a whetstone. She smiled at me. I flinched. The ghouls shrank back; the other creatures from the cemetery watched on, hesitant to come forward. I moved back, slowly, carefully, unsure of how to deal with her.

'Who are you?' I asked, confused.

'Let's just say I handed out justice. He left me for her, I got her to kill him. I ended my life right there, on that knoll, where we'd sat so many nights watching the moon. I took a knife to my wrists and stuck a hanger into my uterus to kill his child in me, and my blood leached into the soil, the blood from my womb, the blood from my wrists, sinking deep, so deep that I became the earth, and I festered and grew. And today he dared come here with her, on the anniversary of me taking my life. To sit exactly at that same spot, to mock my death.'

She smiled again. Knives. Serrated. Her anger, her grief, her venom had turned her into a chudail.

She turned to look at him, putting a hand out to him, her nails talons that dug into his wrist. He recoiled.

'Come, my love. We have an eternity to be together now.'

Above us, the supermoon smiled. Dripping blood.

Catherine McNamara grew up in Sydney and ran away to Paris at 21 to write, and ended up in Ghana, co-running a bar, with detours in Mogadishu and Milan along the way. She has worked as a translator, writing coach, embassy secretary, shoe model, gallery owner, and now lives between the Venice and the Veneto countryside where she mentors writers. She is the author of the collections *The Carnal Fugues*, *The Cartography of Others*, *Love Stories for Hectic People* and *Pelt and Other Stories*, published in the UK and Australia. *The Carnal Fugues* has been shortlisted for the Prime Minister's Awards for Fiction 2024 in Australia. Catherine's short fiction speaks of sensuality and discomfort, of estrangement and desire, and is grounded in a fascination with language and literature itself.

For Catherine, revenge is the inverse of love, an unsteadying of the soul, a dangerous realignment of passion.

9

Three Days in Hong Kong

CATHERINE MCNAMARA

YOU FLY IN. He says he won't be there, there'll be a sign with your code name. *Philomena M.* He likes secrets. You know he likes living between several worlds suspended in the air. He likes flights. He risks collisions. He travels way too much.

There is the card with your secret name. *Philomena M.* The driver has pointed sideburns like Nick Cave and skin pulled tight over his cheekbones.

You drive onto the motorway, into the night, past cheap housing blocks with scabbed façades, balconies crammed as though the life is oozing out of them. The city pulls you in, sucks you under, chucks you up, then streams around you. Chasms, rafts of lights, a Prada shop; the black numb sky and nowhere water.

You pull into a ritzy place. The driver carries your half-empty suitcase, lopsided by books. You see a shabby Caucasian couple, hear them speak Australian.

Your room number is 537. A slim porter manoeuvres your bag.

The room makes you start. It is layers of ruffled smoothness and finally the deep ink panel of the harbour. Buildings corded in light.

You have barely sat down on the loo when the phone rings and you waddle out, knickers around your thighs.

'You've made it then,' he says.

'Well, I was booked,' you reply.

'I can't wait to see you.'

'I'm wet as—'

'I'm full as—'

He is fiddling with something. His phone? His trousers?

'Touch yourself,' he says.

'I am, darling.' You are not.

'I can't make it tonight. Just sit tight. Rest yourself. I'll drop by early tomorrow. I'll wake you up with a little morning attention. Make sure you're naked between those sheets.'

You go to the window. The city is a wide sweep of glitter. In the story of your life, you are lovestruck and yearning, lucky and crazy. But you are not. You feel like laughing when he looms over you. You don't like the *ahh* sound that escapes through his nose after sex. You don't like his bum. You run a bath, trying to imagine his apartment, his groomed wife, the people he employs to keep his life clean. You think he has three young sons.

✥

In the morning you wake up to his phone call. Jet lag.

'I knocked, baby. You didn't answer. I knew you'd be tired after the trip. I nearly came in my trousers outside your door. You make me drown in you. I'm at work now. It's a beautiful day. I'd like to take you out on the harbour.'

You crawl over. You are in Hong Kong. Outside, everything is fumy with light.

'My office is not so far from your hotel. I should be able to pop in later. Don't shower. I want to savour you. I can't believe we're not in grimy London and I have you all to myself.'

You murmur. You hate air travel. You fell asleep with your book on your chest and didn't move all night. You wander over to the bathroom to pee, telephone to your ear. Your mouth is rancid. This room feels bigger than your apartment.

'Why don't you order some fresh fruit? Have them send up something. How I wish I could lather you with mango and papaya, my beauty.'

'I will, darling,' you say.

'That's a weak little kitten talking there.'

'I'll perk up.'

'You've perked me up already. I'll call you later, sweet one.'

You look at yourself in the bathroom mirror. Thirty-seven, no children, you know you are muddling along. And now you've slipped into this crevasse, and you are dangling. The last time you fucked him you told yourself it was glorious. But it was June for Christ's sake, two months back. His friend's place in Highgate. You look at your face beginning to twitch with lines, your still-beautiful eyebrows in high Arabic arches. You think of the man you walked away from, who loved you and went on to marry another woman who bore a disabled daughter. How you felt so guilty over that, as if you were the one who made it happen. You had to be.

✣

After breakfast you are stuffed. A package arrives at the door. You hope they haven't made a mistake and close the door swiftly. It is a Chanel shopping bag with a ribbon. There is the most delightful handbag inside, and you inhale the scent.

The distrustful side of you thinks, *a copy?* as you hunt for the guarantee, some sort of certificate.

It's there all right.

You lounge in front of the television. You switch it off and read your book. You close that and look out at the harbour, which has a hard flat light, not blue like other seas. You wonder if it is a big harbour, or an inlet. You didn't buy a guidebook; he said he would whisper it to you, write it all on your skin.

✧

'You won't believe what's happened. There's been a lot of movement at the office. I've got to put in the hours today. My honey, it's just not going to happen this afternoon, our harbour cruise. Can you hold out? You didn't wash your lovely skin, I hope.'

'I'll let you do that, my darling.'

The long empty hours make you feel a form of love unfurling towards him. Is it the waiting, the stretchy irrelevance of time in this ludicrously luxurious box? You're in love with him for a minute.

'I can't talk any longer. Get yourself a bottle of champagne. I'll help you finish it off. The handbag – it's not too classic, is it? I wouldn't want to label you, my love.'

'It's adorable. You are too good to me.'

You head to the shower.

✧

In the afternoon you doze, and then it is dark again. The day has been upended; it has swept you by. Normally you are such a productive person. This is insane. You feel drugged. Your thick hair is still damp from the shower. Frizzy. Awful. You hang up the three dresses you have brought for the three days, now minus one. You've packed slinky things, things that will slip off your skin, fabrics that will show up its warm sheen. You hope they are not too vulgar. You haven't a clue what people wear here, or where he will take you. You slide on a cobalt blue dress that throws your breasts into relief. You wish your tubby tummy didn't have to show too. You should probably make a visit to the gym downstairs.

An hour before he is meant to pick you up, your phone rings.

'This is totally unexpected. Our anniversary, I'm afraid. It's next week but my wife's sister will be here, and my wife has insisted we celebrate tonight. My darling, I can't risk putting her off. But I've managed to book a table in a restaurant in one of the buildings opposite your hotel. Can you believe it? I'm so close by. I can see you, my lovely.'

You look out. Masses of lights. Layers and layers of cubicles. Some empty, some with people still working. Boats plot the harbour. Planes thread the sky.

'Where? Where are you? I can't see you.'

'My wife has her back to the window. We're in the corner. She's just gone to the ladies.'

You are standing, staring into infinite rooms, infinite faces, infinite lights.

'I don't believe you are out there.'

'You don't believe me?'

'What colour is my dress? What colour are the knickers I am flashing now?'

'Your dress is blue, and you are not wearing knickers.'

You are shocked!

'I cannot speak any more, my darling. Remove that dress.'

You stand naked over Hong Kong, your hands in tepees on the glass, your legs apart. Your hair falls down your back, over your breasts. It is hard to believe anyone is watching you. For him, you touch yourself. You are not very wet. The man you left used to arouse you in a moderate way that you felt was not enough. You would lie awake, your lips to his shoulder. You were so mad he never probed your body hard enough, that you made sure his efforts were in vain.

You want to hug his disabled daughter. You decide that when you go back you will call him and do this.

The next morning you rush to the door naked when you hear a knock. As you unlock the door you feel sweat between your hairless buttocks. Everything has been carefully waxed. Your sex is a peeled fruit. Your fingertips like to wander over the moist skin.

It is a woman in a mauve uniform, holding flowers. You snatch them from her.

You throw them down and go to the bathroom where you look at your parts. They are much more beautiful than the flowers. Then this disgusts you, the way the folds are so prominent. You love to pull a man's cock into you.

You go back to read his note.

I'm being a bore, I realize. Flowers! The most divine ones I could find, for the woman I long to embrace with love and lust.

No signature.

They are too perfect to allow them to gasp to death. You put their severed stems into a cut-glass vase on a bevelled glass table. They are orchids, the saddest of all flowers, but in the vase they spread as though in an embrace. They open to you, and they are flawless.

'My darling! You were so gorgeous last night. I saw the way you touched yourself. So slowly. Your fingers pushing inside. Quite a spectacle you were. I kept asking myself, "What is she thinking up there?" My princess. My lover. My pristine baby. The way you opened yourself. Tell me.'

You breathe in, peering over Hong Kong. Today a grey tapestry, the lights are wounds.

'I was craving you, my love. I wanted to straddle you, feel you pounding inside me, feel your hot release.'

You know there is not much point in saying anything else.

'Have you looked outside, my darling? Have you seen the driving rain? I can't see us on the harbour. Or at the gardens. I'll be over to make love to you as soon as I've finished here. Champagne, my love. I want to drink it from every cleft on your body.'

'Oh, you will,' you assure him, shredding orchid petals. Shredding, shredding.

You commence reading your second book.

'Something's happened.'

He sounds upset. This had better be good, you think.

'It's worse than I thought. I never imagined. Please forgive me.'

'What's happened? How can I help?'

'It's my son, L—. My youngest. Appendicitis. Well, peritonitis, they've just announced. I'm at the hospital right now. He was taken from school in an ambulance. They operated an hour ago.'

'Oh my god!'

'I guess that rules out our afternoon tryst. I can't believe the bad luck we've been having.'

'The important thing is that he's okay. Are you worried?'

'Not at all, these doctors are the best. He's in the best hands possible. My wife's pretty shaken up.'

'Of course. What a shock.'

'But kids spring back quickly.'

'They do. Well, mostly.'

'Sorry?'

'I mean they do.'

You are thinking about your ex's disabled daughter, his rotten wage; the way she won't be springing back any time, ever.

'I love you,' you say. It moves through you, a ghastly compulsion to be tied to him at the bottom of the sea, your lungs a matted filigree.

'I love you too,' he says. You would pay to know what he truly thinks.

'I want you inside of me.'

You hear his breath catch, you feel pathetic. You are testing, pushing. He is whispering to you from a walled-in space where his groaning longings are compressed. You hear the noise of machines and a voice on a loudspeaker. You feel power.

'Come to me afterwards. I need to feel you. We can still make this happen.'

'I will. I'll just get my wife settled. Unfortunately, it might take a while. But I'm with you, *ahh*, I'm with you.'

You wake up, still drowsy, head throbbing. There is an empty bottle of champagne near your pillow and a bright-faced woman looking out from the television screen, talking on mute. A perfect face. Hong Kong harbour is chafed by light.

'My darling.'

'It's my last day. I haven't seen you yet. And I'm leaving this evening.'

You are crying, there is too much riderless emotion within you. Perhaps it's the trip, the displacement. Too much inertia, the jet lag. Too much time studying your face in the mirror, bending and hoisting and scrutinizing the descent of your body. You've never had the time for such corrosive nudity.

'I've come all this way to see you.'

You are falling, you have fallen into this room, this lavish fabrication. And now you haul yourself before the astounding panorama, thinly luminous. Your tears are wet with theatre.

'You've been so patient, so unbelievably patient. L—, my son, had a turn last night. We were down there again. His blood pressure dropped. It all went off-kilter for a moment. It was an emergency but he's okay. The doctors here are the best around, the very best. You understand, don't you?'

You know what is implied there. That, childless, you live in an obscene gulf. You can never know these things.

'I guess you'd understand if you had kids,' he says.

You end the call.

That night you tell the receptionist she can go fuck herself and you are not catching any flight to London. You order champagne, you stand by the dramatic window with its view of light-pocked buildings behind buildings and the harbour heaving in its black bucket.

Naked, quite drunk, you plaster yourself on the window. Rolling your body over and over on the glass.

In the morning the hangover passes quickly, and you feel normal, more like yourself than you've felt in a very long time. The jet lag has gone, and you've eased into this time zone. You dress elegantly and step outside into the city's warm cauldron. You wear a huge horny smile on your face. You are *Philomena M*, and this is your fourth day in Hong Kong.

Rudrakshi Bhattacharjee's (2001–17) collection of short stories, *This Is How It Took Place*, was published by HarperCollins India in 2019. The book won the AutHer Award 2020 for best debut fiction. Rudrakshi attended Stanford University's residential course in creative writing as a fourteen-year-old, and Johns Hopkins University's Engineering Innovation program at fifteen. Her collection of poems *This Place I've Never Been* is published by Atta Galatta.

10

When Carl's Café Closed Its Doors on Me

RUDRAKSHI BHATTACHARJEE

MY MOTHER HAD us banned from my favourite coffee shop when I was ten years old. Carl's Café stood atop the filthy grime-covered road on which I often spied cockroaches that everyone in town pretended not to see, because if the best café in our town was infested, the small number of tourists we got each year would vanish.

We usually lost all our business to Ellway, a town marginally bigger than ours, a few miles closer to the sea. In most ways, Ellway was no different from our town – it had the same kind of beach bums and meth heads populating it, about the same number of small diners and cafés, a handful of branded storefronts. As for us, we had a GAP the entire town was proud of and a hotel I had never set foot in but in front of which my mother and I often stood, in the suffocating sun, ice cream dripping down my chin as we watched the large wooden gates sheltered by palm trees open and close, letting out the largest cars our town had ever witnessed. My mother would wallow in the breeze, purse her lips and smile every so often with hope in her eyes and she'd look down at me with her expression glazed, and I knew she was talking but not really to me when she'd say, 'We have everything!' and laugh joyfully, her voice a gentle murmur resembling the chime of the fake gold bells in Catalina's fashion store. She'd say it so loud sometimes that the bush from behind which we watched the hotel would attract a sudden look of suspicion from the security guard on duty.

Everything changed when Ellway was chosen as the next big beach destination and a Four Seasons opened there. Instantly, even the few road-tripping families we'd grown accustomed to, we lost to Ellway and my mother cried, because if our town didn't have any money, she didn't have any money, and she needed money for the grandeur she loved and cherished and so often tried to recreate in the confinement of our dull lives.

The hotel in our town shut down because nobody had any use for it anymore, and my mother cried for that too. She spoke of how that hotel was the crux of my childhood, the cherry on top of my everyday life, and I didn't have the heart to mention that we'd never even been inside. It wouldn't have mattered anyway; my mother never heard anything she didn't want to hear.

And then everything got worse. My father, my mother and I lived in a small, quarantined neighbourhood, and our house had two rooms and a kitchen. It was covered in pesky houseflies, but my mother persevered and promised that one day we'd move into a real house and be real people. She worked double shifts at the diner next door, and charmed anyone who tipped her regularly, because my mother could be quite charismatic; it was the lilt in her voice anytime she spoke, it sounded like she had something worth saying, like you were worth saying something to. She made it sound like she didn't belong in our town, as if she was something more, and she made it sound like you were too. Everyone wanted to sit in her section of the diner, just to hear her speak.

My father never worked – he spent all his time outside the house, and it would be days, weeks and sometimes even months before we even had dinner together. He didn't know my favourite colour and I never bothered to tell him. I didn't know where he went all day or what he was doing, but I knew my mother knew because sometimes she'd call him and scream into the phone, and I would hear laughter on the other end – not only a male voice, but a female one as well. And then, a week after the closing of the hotel, my father took his packed bags, gave my mother one last kiss, nodded to me and walked out with a woman who lived in the building opposite ours. (Sometimes I'd see her at eleven in the night, sitting on the sidewalk with her only pair of wobbly high-heeled boots by her side, smoking.) Later, my mother grudgingly told me that they'd gone to Ellway to start a new life.

I wanted to ask why, why did Daddy leave us, but I knew if I asked my mother, her face would crack and she'd cry for hours, so I didn't say anything and my mother didn't say anything, and the next day she went to work, and she smiled and laughed and chattered with the crowd, but nobody noticed that her eyes were lifeless and her laugh too high-pitched to be genuine. Everything seemed exactly as it'd always been, except it wasn't.

Three days after my father left, my mother was told to take a paid holiday due to the rough patch she was going through. She'd smiled and looked at me and said, as if sensibly, 'It's not really going to be any different,' and I'd smiled back because she was right. I'd rarely seen my father before he'd left, and I was never going to see him again. That woman could have him (maybe he'd buy her a new pair of heeled boots which didn't wobble as much) as long as I had my mother.

My mother told me she'd take me out for a treat, and we'd go to a big fancy restaurant and order an entrée, a main, a side dish, a dessert, and we'd tip the waiters and wear our best dresses and act like celebrities. Of course, I knew that meant she'd wear her new lipstick, and we'd go to any coffee shop nearby and order an extra cupcake.

My mother didn't know that though. She really believed her own lies, and when we walked out of our shoebox of a house towards my favourite coffee shop, I was ecstatic, as was the nature of a ten-year-old girl allured by food, and I didn't pay attention to how my mother's eyes glazed over as we settled down in the familiar embrace of the chairs of Carl's Café, and how a desperate, vicious grin appeared on her cracking face. Her fingers sparked as she leafed through the menu, and when I finally ordered a large steak and ice cream (my mother refused to order; another thin-lipped smile, the condescending 'no, thank you' that put people off), she hissed at me, and I finally saw the rising fire in her eyes.

I remembered listening to my parents arguing once, my father's bellowing, raging voice, my mother's tear-filled words of martyrdom. My father was angry because some of the townies had heard my mother say that this town was a 'waste of space in the middle of nowhere producing idiots who only know how to make bigger idiots', and my mother had defended herself by saying that she was destined for more, that fate would lead her to a life of luxury one day, and my father had sighed and stopped screaming and said, 'Don't you get it? You might not think so, but you're a part of this town, you're one of the idiots.'

And the fire would rise in my mother's eyes any time she wanted to prove him wrong. She was obviously bitter about this issue because my father (the heavy-boned no-brainer) had made it out of here, and she, the elegant one of the two with her fancy accents and great expectations, was still stuck.

The first question out of my mother's mouth was not the one I was expecting. It was only a build-up; I could tell from the nervous frenzy in her voice as she spoke that she was leading up to something. 'Who do you think is prettier, *she* or me?' My mother sat up straight. The real answer was *she*, for *she* was younger, and her hair was blacker, and her nails were longer, and her face was always painted. But that wasn't completely true, because even though my mother's face had creases and she always looked tired and weary, there was a certain class and grace my mother possessed that *she* would never be able to replicate. My mother always seemed magical, something more.

'You, obviously.'

'Would you do anything for me, anything for your

mother? It would be fun, great fun!' My mother's face shone, and the fire started to grow larger and larger.

I swallowed, waited.

'Do you want to do something unscrupulous, something, oh, something simply and utterly debauched?'

I began to eat my steak faster. I wanted to finish it in time.

'Come away then, come away, come, follow me.' There wasn't time to finish the meat because my mother had already pulled me out of Carl's Café and into her world.

We stood in the bushes till closing time when the last waitress locked up and left. Bugs sat in my hair and mosquitoes reddened my calves, and I was sure we had been standing in trash. It was eleven, and there was no one in sight and the streetlights hung miserably in the sudden cold, harsh wind. They flickered on and off and my mother once again pulled me out and in front of the glass doors of Carl's Café.

The fire in my mother's eyes was at the fiercest it had ever been. She also looked the happiest she'd been in a long time. I could see large grey stones at her feet and instantly I knew what she wanted to do. I also knew that there was no point in even trying to stop her. There, on the eve of our banishment from my favourite coffee shop, my mother delivered her soliloquy in pitches of glee and wonder. Her teeth chattered as she spoke in the cold, but the fire in her mind warmed her thoughts.

'We're going to get out if it's the last thing we do. I'll give you a nice life, I promise. One day we'll be real people, in a large mansion with stone-clad walls and a big pool. You like water, don't you? Never mind, I'll hire you ten swimming instructors. Oh, and I'll take you to the centre of my glitz and my glamour, and now this is how we get there. We get out of this town, we make sure they throw us out, I'll get us thrown out, my girl, I'll force us to leave. Just you wait and watch what your mother is made of.'

Then she picked up the gathered stones and flung them at the glass walls, which stood almost ironically in front of us. The glass shattered, and I had a few measly throws too, but it was my mother who threw rock after rock, tears streaming down her face, tears of happiness, tears of joy, and I knew she was once again seeing that which wasn't there. The clanging of the glass, the smashing of its shards on the ground, wasn't as voluminous as I'd expected the downfall to be; it was a distant murmur, a background to the rage inside my mother, the rage of unfulfilled dreams. My mother appropriated the glass walls with the power of the fear that she was destined for nothing, she blazed her desperate pleas for greatness, she heaved tiring failure and disappointment, and I stood, a silent observer, but a follower in the night.

There were no alarms that went off (we weren't as fancy as that), but after a hazy ten minutes, Carl appeared screaming, and my mother fainted, and I watched and fainted too.

✣

When we were revived, it was morning. My mother looked as contained and sophisticated as she always did, so much so that I could hardly believe anything had even happened the night before. I'd thought, in the illusion of the darkness of the night, that we'd completely trashed Carl's Café, and that it had disintegrated completely, but later I learned that we'd barely broken a part of the glass. Still, even though Carl wasn't taking us to the police, we had been caught doing something we weren't supposed to, something so barbarous that my mother had laughed when Carl had confronted her.

He was furious and told her that she'd made a terrible mistake and that the town would turn its back on her, and that the only refuge she'd find would be outside the town limits, and he told her that he wanted her to leave and never come near his café again.

✣

Looking back, if we hadn't been caught the day my mother decided to rebel, I would probably be a waitress working at the same café I'd once set out to destroy. And for the sake of complete honesty, I'm glad we got caught because my mother was right; having the town hate us and turn us out was the best thing to ever happen to us because it forced us to leave. It forced us to start over, it forced us to try for the greatness my mother only ever dreamt about.

Looking back, I am glad I was only ten years old when my mother had us banned from my favourite coffee shop, because I was still young, and my mother made sure I didn't grow up a dead end.

Anukrti Upadhyay has post-graduate degrees in management and literature, and a graduate degree in law. Her doctoral thesis was on human relationships in Hindi short stories of the post-1960s. She writes fiction and poetry in both English and Hindi. Her English works, twin novellas *Daura* and *Bhaunri*, and novel *Kintsugi*, have received award nominations, and she has been awarded the Sushila Devi Award for the best work of fiction written by a woman author in 2020 for *Kintsugi*. Her latest work is the short-story collection *The Blue Women*. Her Hindi works include short-story collection *Japani Sarai* and novel *Neena Aunty*. Her writings have appeared in *Scroll.in*, Kitaab.org, the *Bombay Review*, the *Bangalore Review* and several Hindi publications.

She has worked for global investment banks Goldman Sachs and UBS in senior positions and now works with Wildlife Conservation Trust. She divides her time between Mumbai and the rest of the world, and when not counting trees and birds, she can be found ingratiating herself with every child, cat and dog in her vicinity.

To her, revenge is a collective failure to ensure mechanisms for safe, effective and just redressals; it is victims choosing violence, cunning and harm out of desperation and anger; it is society's unhealing wound.

11

Vibha

ANUKRTI UPADHYAY

ALIGHTING FROM THE bus, Vibha could see the frosted-glass door, with the firm's name embossed in ice-blue lettering, suspended above the dusty street cool, mysterious, a magic portal guarding a sanctuary.

The design firm Vibha worked for – by Bappa's blessings, as her mother never failed to add, pulling her ears to ward off the evil eye – wasn't big but it had carved out a niche for itself with minimalist designs, a light colour palette and striking art pieces sourced from countries whose names Vibha had never heard. We are proud of the work we do, our style is international, cosmopolitan, it starts conversations, the firm's co-founder had said over a Zoom call from her home in Dubai, the dizzying, dazzling city-skyline framed in the window behind her distracting Vibha, people might say that doing interiors is a rich woman's hobby and, sure, our first clients were friends and family but we have built a business for ourselves, we have clients in Mumbai, Dubai and London, we are profitable, we have an ethos – we only hire women, we give opportunities to freelancers, we are completely egalitarian, no hierarchy, no big-small-high-low, you can call or email anytime you like, ask questions, discuss ideas, even our office is open-plan, no doors.

Money, profit, capitalism, add to it nepotism, no fucks given for feminism, the junior designer had chanted after the call. The junior and senior designers as well as the head of marketing were all related to the Dubai-based founder, who also owned the low-rise building that housed the firm's office. The open-door speech is hokum too, the junior designer warned Vibha, don't call her unless she calls you first and never ever send her anything without showing it to us first.

There's a process, the senior designer had offered, process is important.

Process-shmocess, the junior designer had tossed her helmet towards the hook on the wall, it's called hierarchy.

The senior designer's eloquent eyebrows had flickered up and down. They were the most beautiful eyebrows Vibha had ever seen, dark and arched like bird wings, rising in a perfect wave from nose bridge to temples. She had learnt later that a woman flew in from Delhi every month to attend to the eyebrows of the fastidious women of Bombay. An eyebrow artist like none other, the junior designer had said, with a price tag like none other too!

To Vibha, the senior and junior designers were fantastical creatures. They both had glossy hair, foreign degrees and unfamiliar accents, but were different in other ways. The senior designer, with those wondrous eyebrows and a sing-song way of speaking, an occasional Hindi word rising like an effervescent bubble in the silver flow, was from the city, born and brought up in one of the old, elegant buildings along the sea, not far from Worli Naka, where Vibha herself grew up. She was devoted to her toy-like curly-haired dog – my baby jaan, my messy goofball, can't tell his nose from his toes but super sweet.

The junior designer's curly-haired dog was folk arts, climate change and, as she put it, 'not giving a fuck', she rode an electric scooter, sported a strawberry pink helmet with a yellow-haired Marilyn Monroe cheekily winking at the world, and said fuck a lot. She was born and raised in America and fashioned objects from a mixture of clay, straw and jaggery, materials she termed traditional. The objects she made – book holders shaped like a pair of moon-like buttocks, wall hooks like a hand with the middle finger raised – perplexed and confused Vibha. They weren't beautiful to her and yet she found it difficult to look away. My way of saying make art and fuck climate deniers, she said to Vibha, by the way I am relying on you to teach me about the art from your village. She brushed aside Vibha's explanation of being born in Worli Naka and never having been farther than Thane in her life. You've access to traditional design knowledge through the women in your family, she insisted, your mother, your grandmother, your aunts. Vibha did not contradict her, did not say that her mother too was raised in Mumbai, in a slum not far from the one she herself was born in, that the only traditional knowledge her grandmother, visiting occasionally from the village in Ratnagiri, a two-day journey by tempo–bus–auto, shared was that of traditional injustices – of the village sarpanch, the tehsildar, the block development officer colluding to allow neighbours to encroach on their meagre land. Instead, Vibha wondered silently at the junior designer navigating the crowded streets of the city on her little scooter, dressed in flimsy crop tops and rainbow leggings. How did she manage with the men on the streets, with their impudent gaze, their lewd comments that Vibha herself weathered every day, even without bare shoulders and an exposed midriff? Perhaps the streets were different for her and for the senior designer, who arrived in a chauffeur-driven car the colour of watered tea and crossed the street negligently, looking neither left nor right, expecting the autos and motorcycles to manoeuvre around her.

The public bus Vibha took each day from Worli Naka to the office in the quiet residential lane in Khar, wove in and out of the congested neighbourhoods of Dadar and Mahim before emerging on the broad and busy Linking Road. All along the way, clouds of dust and smoke blew in through the windows jammed open for air. The acrid, spoilt smells of the sea and the earth under stress from reclamations and excavations assailed her; the cacophony of horns, sirens, whistles, shouts, the ebb and flow of relentlessly hard lives battered her; every day she felt the city tremble and writhe under the assaults of earthmovers, concrete-mixers, motograters. Under the detritus of endurance and endeavour, Vibha felt a crust form over her, enveloping her entirely, hardening moment by moment till she was trapped, unable to breathe freely.

Alighting from the bus, Vibha crossed the street with stiff steps, shoulders held tight, neck bent. The staircase smelt of the lemony pet shampoo the pet grooming parlour on the ground floor used. It tickled her nostrils, her shell-like crust loosened in anticipation of the silent harmony of the unpeopled office, a cool refreshing wash in the spotless bathroom, puffs of Pond's face powder applied liberally and, finally, a quiet cup of tea beside the window, gazing at the pedestrians sweating in the hot street below. For these two hours, the office, its closed-up pristine quietude belonged to her alone.

However, all this had changed in the past few days. As Vibha unlocked the door and stepped into the trapped coolness of yesterday's air-conditioning, the corners of her mouth fell. There was the hot hiss of the gas stove in the kitchen, the rush of a running tap, the slap of feet on tiles, signs of the new cleaner's unceasing presence.

The cleaner himself stuck his head out of the kitchen door, the sticky sickly-sweet smell of milk and sugar boiling together, escaping into the sterile office space. 'Chaha pahije?' he asked.

Vibha heaved the backpack off her shoulders, her long-cheeked, demure-eyed face passive. Her mother was proud of her looks and often pointed out her resemblance to Nutan, a Bollywood actress of the 1960s. 'No...' she shook her head, busily switching on the twin LCD screens that displayed the firm's projects, rooms and offices alternating with cool-toned visuals of fields of mauve and violet flowers – Vibha had difficulty believing such flowers existed in reality despite assurances by the junior designer that she had shot them herself in Japan. 'Busy day...' she muttered, breathing shallowly.

'It is ready, I just made for myself, sweet tea, hot-hot, I can easily spare a cupful,' the new cleaner sniggered. 'My steel tumbler is equal to three of your chini-mitti cups.'

Vibha kept her head averted, avoiding looking at his eyebrow-less face with its bulging, oily cheeks and an uncertain mouth lurking under scant facial hair, its one twisted eye permanently pointing inwards in a severe squint. But she could not avoid the smell as he came closer, the smell of stale sweat trapped under armpits and in between toes hastily scrubbed at a communal tap, of imperfectly dried clothes worn while still damp, of bodies squished together in humid heat. Dipping down, she opened and closed the drawers of her desk noisily, slipping her plastic outdoor sandals under the desk and retrieving the pale green soft-soled shoes she wore in the office. The shoes were manufactured in a factory owned by the senior designer's father, and several pairs were stacked in a show shoe-shelf. See if a pair fits you, the senior designer had suggested, you can wear them around the office, they go with the colour scheme here. Though she hadn't said anything about Vibha's sandals, browned by dust, the strap patched up and sewn together, Vibha had seen her glance in their direction. The junior designer had agreed enthusiastically – yup, Vibs, do that, those shoes may not be the height of fashion but at least they won't squeal like dying mice every time you step on these porcelain tiles, which, to be honest, are more suitable for a swank bog than an office. The tiles are handmade in Spain, the senior designer had pronounced, her eyebrows moving slightly. Right, the junior designer shrugged, I did say swank.

'I can bring it right out...' The cleaner stepped closer.

Breathing shallowly, Vibha continued to root among the drawers. 'Upvaas...' she said without emerging, 'can't eat...'

'Not even tea? Nirjal upvaas?' the new cleaner exclaimed. 'Very tough...' He retreated to the kitchen. Vibha noticed that he wore the same pale-green, soft-soled shoes. She straightened and, reaching up, pressed the button on the room-freshener. It dispensed an extra puff of cool floral fragrance.

Technically, it wasn't the cleaner but Vibha who was new. She had joined the company three months ago after finishing a diploma course in graphic design. The diploma and this job had both come to her through a tenuous chain of chances, the boon of good luck that her mother was so proud and so fearful of. At the other end of the skein of lucky chances that connected her to this richly white, softly fragrant office was a plastic cone filled with olive-coloured mehndi paste, a bare palm and her ability to produce intricate ornate patterns from imagination.

Vibha had applied mehndi on the palms of women in

her neighbourhood as far back as she could remember. Every arrival of Ganpati, every anticipation of the Eid moon found her bent over hands and feet, lost in joyous designs. By the time she was in high school, she was going as far as Tardeo to the south and Kurla to the north to participate in mehndi competitions. Cone in hand, she forgot everything, her attention retreated inwards, and detailed patterns emerged spontaneously – winged horses, dancing peacocks, wedding parties complete with horses and palkis. At one such competition, the woman judging it was struck by the fantastical scenes Vibha had conjured up. She turned out to be the director of a city NGO and a friend of the design firm's founder. You are talented, she declared, I will find a way to lift you out of all this.

'All this' encompassed Vibha's life as she had known it so far. It included her invalid alcoholic father, who had acquired an unhealing wound one hot April day when a piece of metal he was pushing through a die-cutting machine fell on his leg, slicing it to the bone; her mother, who worked several utensil-scrubbing, sweeping, swabbing jobs in the condominiums across the road and bought a quart of daaru for her husband every evening, humming 'Krishnacha Radhecha'; her two noisy brothers, who demanded something or the other all the time – tea, snacks, help with homework. It also included the transit building – a tall, narrow block of one-room dwellings – which was Vibha's home ever since the slum facing the seashore, where she had been conceived and birthed, was demolished to make way for a luxury apartment complex. The block was a temporary arrangement, the builder had sworn by Jari Mari Mata, whose temple in the middle of the slum had to be demolished as well; the residents were to get modern apartments with running water, indoor toilets and elevators and the un-housed deity an airconditioned temple within a matter of months. It was now over twenty years since that promise, and most of the residents of the transit block, or Transy as they called it, had accepted the ten-by-ten cells they referred to as their homes. Transy had aged poorly; its outside was streaked with mould, the paint on the inner walls bubbled and flaked, and the stairwells were spattered with betel-juice and crude graffiti and smelt of urine. The corridor along which Vibha and her family had their room grew danker and dingier with every monsoon, its ceiling radiating cracks. Sounds filled it, flowing out of open doors and through flimsy walls, sounds of sewing machines and embroidery machines, pressure cookers and televisions, of the thousand human lives jostling and rubbing against each other, piled and stuffed and packed together in the ten stories of Transy – fighting, singing, lovemaking, dying.

The room Vibha and her family lived in was divided into two halves, an old saree strung from a clothesline serving as partition. In the curtained half lay her father in an alcoholic drowse, groaning and cursing his wound, the piece of metal that had injured him and god. In the other half, the rest of the family did all their living – cooking, eating, squabbling, sleeping. The room always reeked. It reeked of pus and decay, of stale food and bodies, the smell intense and all-encompassing, like something that ferments and decays before it ripens. Layered over the sounds of the streets and the Transy, was the snoring, belching, muttering, grunting, sleep-talking of the family. There was no respite, no escape. Night and day, ceaselessly, the sounds and smells pressed upon Vibha, heavy, inert, deadening like a scar tissue.

The first time Vibha entered the design firm's office she felt a quickening. That such perfumed precincts – pearly milk-frothy unsullied floral fragrant fresh soft cushioned silent – could exist in the sweaty stale fervid grimy gritty noisy crudeness of the city had struck her mute. She nodded and stammered monosyllabic replies as the junior designer showed her around the large, open-plan office, organized like a box-within-a-box, each box with three sides. When Vibha left at the end of that first day, the bus with its tired crowd of heavy-eyed men and women with wilted flowers in their hair, the noise and smells of the crowded hot streets, the squalor and dirt in the unpaved compound of Transy, left her shaken and disoriented. At night, after the rest of the household slept, she and her mother stuck glittery crystals and spangles on diaphanous lengths of chiffon that the trader from Masjid Bunder brought once every fortnight and paid the women thirty rupees per piece to embellish. Tired yet restless, her mother began talking about her day – the ill-health of one of her employers, the old TV set another had promised to give her on Diwali, the excellent pumpkin, only slightly, very slightly, overripe that she had cleverly managed to snag from the vegetable vendor at half price. Vibha felt her body grow heavy, sinking helplessly into the stinking morass of the Transy and its warren-like homes, their sweaty exhaustion, their meagre eagerness.

Her second day at work, the senior designer found Vibha sitting on the stairs, backpack beside her, waiting. Her eyebrows leapt when she learnt that Vibha had arrrived hours ago. She unlocked the office and handed the keys to Vibha – keep the keys, I never come before eleven anyway. Vibha received the keys like a blessing. From then on, the rhythm of her day was set: she took the earliest bus, was the first to arrive at the office, was the first to unlock the cool opaque door, the first to glide into the still sanctuary, the first to bathe in the lingering fragrances, the first to clothe herself in the silken strands of silence. Entirely alone for the first time in all her twenty-one years, in the unbroken solitude of those morning hours, she experienced a kind of easing, a release at the center of her being.

Vibha enjoyed the work she did at the office; there was an evenness, a smoothening predictability to it despite everything being novel, unfamiliar. She did freehand drawings of objects and materials for concept books and occasionally for live projects. The senior and junior designers took turns to teach her to use the design software, drawing and editing tools, read and understand architecture blueprints and maps. Being utterly unaware of her desperation, they were impressed by her will to learn, her quickness to grasp. You are freaking talented, Vibs, the junior designer told her as Vibha presented a three-dimensional sketch of a chandelier in a concept home, just don't be so unsure of yourself, go bold or go home is the team motto here. The chandelier had arrived and was on display in the conference room, its coloured glass spirals moving and twisting in the draught from the air-conditioner, throwing variegated shadows on the walls. It reminded Vibha of the tinsel buntings in the Ganesh pandal at Transy. Only without the din, she observed shyly to the junior designer one day. Vibs, you clever girl, the junior designer said, this piece is named Celebration, and it is by a Native American artist who will be famous any day now. Vibha marvelled at the confidence with which the junior designer pronounced the future. Her own certainties were limited to her inescapable home, the chaos and crowd of Transy. Slowly, hesitantly, she added the office, its smooth, iridescent, shell-like solitude to those certainties.

Occasionally, the office was stirred by the visit of the founders. The arrival of the founder from Dubai was predictable – she arrived straight from the airport, matching pieces of beautiful metallic silvery luggage and crisp cardboard boxes of varied shapes, marked 'samples', in tow. She gave quick hugs to senior and junior designers and the marketing head, nodded to Vibha and the itinerant band of freelance graphic artists who flowed in and out of the office, and rushed to the conference room to huddle with the head of marketing and occasionally with the senior and junior designers while the pastries and chocolates she had picked up at some airport or the other were distributed around. Not too long after arriving, she left – for site visits, client meetings and other mysterious activities. The other founder's visit was far more dramatic – a muscly man in a dark safari suit opened the office door one late afternoon and stood aside. A woman entered, a woman the likes of whom Vibha hadn't seen – her flowing peachy-pink draperies matched her buttery-pink complexion, she held herself like a pitcher of water, laboriously, carefully, she had long, kohl-lined sleepy eyes which she slanted around before parting her taut, pouting lips to pronounce a general greeting in a voice like gently crackling paper. Her long, glossy tresses glinted red and copper. Wig, the senior designer mouthed, catching Vibha's astonished eye.

Botox, baby, botox, the junior designer sang after she left, capsules, vials, syringes of fucking botox.

The senior designer's dainty eyebrows moved slightly. She's the face of the firm, she commented.

A face lifted, tightened, filled and injected, the junior designer sang, twisting her waist and bottom and tapping her feet in an improvised dance.

Whatever, she's the one who gets us in lifestyle mags and on celebrity projects through her Bollywood connects.

Yeah, that Bollywood connect, the junior designer winked, she was the girlfriend of like a really old-time movie star. Don't know the whole story but there were lots of rumours because the dude died suddenly while they were on a vacay in Europe...

No one knows the whole story, the senior designer observed, that's part of her mystique.

Is she called Celebration too, Vibha asked daringly.

She is actually a former celebration, the senior designer quipped back, by the way, she noticed you, she said you look like some actress from eons ago.

Vibha blinked. Nutan, she said, she was famous when my mother was young.

Yes, Nutan, that's the name she mentioned, apparently, she once produced a movie starring this Nutan chick.

Produced a movie with Nutan, Vibha's eyes rounded. That must be fifty years ago, and the founder, with her perfumed roundness and shiny skin, must be decades older than her mother. An image rose before Vibha's eyes – her mother crouched in a corner, mashing the overripe pumpkin, unmindful of a yellow smear of pulp drying on her shrivelled cheek, her frizzy thinning hair surrounding her sunken face in a dusty aura while the unspeakable smell of dirty rags that never quite dry mingled with that of the overblown vegetable. Vibha felt the bile rise in her throat and inwardly counted the number of hours she had left in the white, pristine, softly perfumed office.

✥

The new cleaner was mentioned for the first time by the marketing head a couple of weeks after the celebrity founder's visit. Vibha was drawing a bookshelf using the design stencil tool. For a woman's den, the junior designer had explained, if men can have man caves, why shouldn't women have exclusive woman dens?

Vibha had hidden her incomprehension by focusing on the drawing.

I can never share my space, the marketing head had volunteered, not with anybody, my space is sacrosanct. By the way, Tiloki will be back next week.

His wife has popped? The senior designer had cocked an eyebrow.

Yes, a boy after three girls.

It is only in India that someone who looks like Big Man T can find a wife and produce kids, the junior designer said. She was looking over Vibha's shoulder; good job, Vibs, now drag the planter and drop it to the right of the bookshelf.

Play nice, the marketing head admonished, he's been with our family since he was a kid, his mother worked for us, his father too when he wasn't drinking. He might not be the sharpest knife, but he is super honest and does what he's told.

I am not complaining, the junior designer had raised her hands, I am happy that we'll have a functioning pantry again. The dude makes fucking good sandwiches.

I can't stand the soft toast he makes and the amount of butter he slathers on, the senior designer's eyebrows expressed her dismay.

Why would you? You have a fancy-shmancy maharaj to make elaborate lunches with quinoa and avocados and nut butter, the junior designer taunted, ask Vibs what she'd like better – a freshly made Bombay sandwich a la Tiloki or cold roti from home.

Immersed in working on the design of the woman den, Vibha had not realized the significance of the return of the cleaner and, therefore, a few days later, upon unlocking the office, she was confused by the unmistakable smell of boiling milk with its notes of soured sweetness and heated fats. The new cleaner had looked out of the kitchen, casting a negligent glance at her cotton kurta, her rainproof backpack, her sweaty face. Later he had brought her a cup of tea. Badi madam ji told me, he held out the cup, she said a new designer has come and I thought – someone hi-fi from London-Paris. He had chuckled, his eyes retreating into the folds of his cheeks, his belly quivering. A familiar smell rose from him. Her mind in chaos, Vibha fixed her eyes on the screen of her laptop.

By the time the senior and junior designers arrived, the tea in the cup on Vibha's desk had turned cold and stale under a brown crinkly skin. The senior designer had raised an eloquent eyebrow towards the kitchen and wrinkled her nose slightly.

Big Man T, the junior designer had called out cheerily, welcome back and all. The baby arrived safely? All's well with the wife?

The cleaner emerged from the kitchen, a carboard box of milk sweets in hand. A boy, he said his mouth askew in a proud smile, not named yet, forty days got over only last week, have some burfi, madam ji.

A boy, huh, sorry to hear, the junior designer said mischievously, never mind, maybe you'll get lucky and have another girl next time.

The cleaner bit his tongue and pulled at the lobes of his ears to ward off such an evil wish, no, no, madam ji, three girls already, no more, no more.

The senior designer turned her glossy ponytail and gleaming nape towards the room. Tiloki, she ordered, please switch on the exhaust fan in the pantry and keep the door closed at all times, and make sure the flower arrangements are not jumbled when you change the water.

Yeah, and don't get your wife pregnant again either, let the poor woman live, the junior designer added.

The cleaner giggled, lowering his tiny eyes, crooked and straight, and retreated to the kitchen.

I wonder what the poor kid looks like, the junior designer sighed.

I don't, the senior designer said in the tone that was like her arched eyebrow.

Vibha said nothing. She waited for the evening, when the cleaner would leave and the office would be restored to its silence. Perhaps then the broken rhythm of her day could be reconjured. She could make a cup of tea, drink it slowly looking down at the street, erase the cleaner with his squint eyes and his cleaned-up slum smell and his four child-replicas, like a bunch of baby slugs hanging from the hermaphrodite parent slug she had once seen in a nature documentary. She could make the quiet space her own again. She waited for the evening to inflate her lungs fully and breathe freely.

The evening fell but the new cleaner showed no signs of leaving. Instead, he puttered around the office, pulling down blinds, straightening chairs, opening and shutting cupboards, breathing noisily, shuffling his feet, complaining about the dust accumulated in the creases and corners. All the blinds are dusty, he muttered importantly, posies of dust everywhere, I will have to clean everything top to bottom, those people from the cleaning company are just lazy, kamchors all of them. Vibha stiffened, something hot and sharp-edged pressed against her. She quietly slipped the milk sweet from the morning, sticky with sugar-sweat, into the bin and turned off her computer.

The senior designer looked up and raised a questioning eyebrow.

That's a first, the junior designer hooted, Vibs leaving at 6 p.m. Dollars to doughnuts, our girl has a date tonight!

Vibha sat on the stained metal bench at the bus stop and waited. Bus after bus halted and passed, heading to different parts of the town – Kurla, Dharavi, Worli Naka. She sat absolutely still, holding herself rigid, watching the street with abstracted eyes. At last, the cleaner emerged from the office building and set out. Vibha rose and with quick steps crossed the street. Unlocking the office door, she stepped in and stopped dead – there, right in front of the glass conference room with its egg-shell enamel table and fragile chairs and framed photographs of arctic plants in bloom, upon the beautiful ivory-on-alabaster tiles featured in the *Indian Journal of Design*, was a thin grey mattress and a pillow in a greasy case, not unlike the ones in her home in Transy. A red-blue plastic bottle, the colour of a poisoned wound, stood next to the mattress. Vibha's throat constricted and eyes brimmed over. She closed the door and headed towards the bus stop.

✣

Vibha still took the early bus from home but the joy that had suffused her as she sat crowded, jolted and jostled three to a seat, jolted and jostled, vanished. Her mornings now were tea-less, solitude-less, their calm tempo destroyed. Some days she found the cleaner still asleep on his mattress, bottles of local alcohol lying beside it, the office reverberating with the sound of his snores, or padding around shirtless, his eyes bloodshot, protruding belly hanging over a frayed pair of cotton shorts, pale and hairless like the insides of the carcasses in butcher's shops. Every inch of the office smelt of his clothes, his food, his flesh.

Tiloki sleeps in the office, Vibha ventured one day, sometimes he is still asleep when I get in, he doesn't wear a shirt...

Oh gosh, poor Vibs, the junior designer put an arm around her shoulders, you've seen the great effing gut too! You are now part of a hopefully small though utterly horror-struck sorority!

The senior designer's eyebrows did a dainty little dance. His family lives somewhere far, in one of those funny sounding 'burbs, Diva, I think, he goes home only every Sunday.

Poor T, spending the entire week in here, the junior designer sighed, must be tough on him.

Vibha lowered her eyes, the office is so beautiful, she said, anyone would like to stay...

The junior designer shook her head. Not me, too fucking sterile for me, I like my small perch down the road, it's not some humongous-sized mansion like hers, she wagged her head towards the senior designer, but it's cozy and it's mine.

The senior designer agreed. If you really think about it, staying here is a real hardship, his family isn't here, he's all alone after the day's work, no one to talk to or unwind with. Tell him to wear clothes though, this isn't his personal space.

Vibha swallowed the bitterness in her mouth. Hardship meant a cramped room next to an open drain in Diva, it meant wallowing in the humid heat, in the smells of milk, damp cloth diapers and sewage, jolting awake at the clatter of a train passing on the tracks nearby and being kept awake the rest of the night by the wails of an infant. It did not mean watching item songs featuring half-clad women on the 51-inch LCD screen in the reception after chugging daaru. But she said nothing.

Vibha took to slipping quietly into the office in the mornings and going straight to her desk, head down, eyes lowered. She stopped walking across to the drafting desk beside the picture window to look with shy curiosity at the blueprint the senior or junior designer were working on. She stopped smiling at the junior designer's jokes or at the latest cleverness of the senior designer's toy-dog. She ventured into the kitchen only when the cleaner stepped out on an errand or to smoke the beedi tucked behind his ear. The familiar turgid, stale, soured-milk odours in the kitchen agitated her like old disappointments and she hastily went through the motions of tea-making, dropping tea leaves into the pot without waiting for the water to come to a boil. Even so, the cleaner occasionally returned before she was done. Vibha watched helplessly as he brought the tea to a boil again and again like her mother and strained it directly into the cup, allowing brown droplets to splash and stain the cup's smooth beautiful white glaze. The feeling of oppression, of being thwarted, of something exquisite being taken away trailed into her nights. Her restless brain lay awake even as her body fell into an uneasy slumber, like a nestling in an unsafe nest, the nightly sounds of snores, groans, farts, moans, her father's gruff call to her mother, her mother's suffering sighs, pressed against her taut, aching consciousness. Dull and tired from a lack of restful sleep, she sometimes dozed off on the bus, her head drooping, only to recoil from the rubbery moist touch of a sweaty shoulder smelling of coconut oil and garlic, even as the owner of the shoulder, usually a woman with flowers in her hair and neatly pinned saree, smiled reassuringly.

Only the junior designer remarked on the changes in Vibha. You are becoming all work and no play, Vibs, no tea-breaks, no smile-breaks, no breaks from serious-work-face. No snack breaks either, you didn't even try the yummy Shrewsbury biscuits from the cool old Iranian cafe near Mahalakshmi.

It was true. Not just the tea, Vibha declined everything the cleaner served – dosa bought from the stall down the road that he expertly crisped on the griddle in the kitchen, the sandwiches he painstakingly made, one good eye narrowed in concentration, the snacks he carefully served, his thick fingers handling the food deftly.

But she couldn't decline his confidences. Every morning after finishing his tasks he emerged from the kitchen, pale worms of fingers wrapped around his steel tumbler of tea, and resumed the conversation from the previous day. With Vibha he was garrulous about troubles he never mentioned to the senior or junior designers. troubles he never mentioned to the senior or junior designers. My wife is still poorly, he said one morning, sucking noisy mouthfuls of tea, she is not getting her maahvari on time, the doctor says she must eat two eggs daily-daily, must not lift buckets and things, he might as well say she isn't allowed to be a poor man's wife. No mard-aurat hanky-panky, he says, tell me how can a mard be denied his own wife, it is an old problem he says, takes time he says, motherfucking how long? It has been weeks. The bachcha-rok dhibri inside her is causing trouble, he says, then take out the behencho... but no, there's pus, buy this medicine, buy that medicine, he says, I have paid him 500 five times but still pus behencho... Heat rose in a wave inside Vibha. Gagging, she ran, her mouth teeth jaw clenched hard. In the washroom, all alone among the softly glowing surfaces of stone and porcelain, the exhaust whirring soothingly, she retched and retched in the toilet bowl till she felt light-headed.

Are you alright, the new cleaner called from outside, you need Pudin Hara?

Upon learning about the attack of nausea, the senior designer insisted that Vibha see a doctor. You might have food poisoning, I got it once when I ate at this seafood joint in Dadar, her eyebrows knitted in pained remembrance, it seemed an okay kind of place, someone from my group of friends had been there before, but oh my god what it did to me... I almost died. You must go to your doctor and then go home and rest.

Yeah, that's true, the junior designer chimed in, there's nothing like pulling down the blinds and lying in your own bed quietly when you aren't well, you know.

Vibha looked at the two of them, they were both at the drafting desk by the window and seemed to emit the light they stood in. If she described the dim corridor reverberating with the shrill whistles of pressure cookers and cries of children, leading to the room with the sick groaning drunkard in one corner, the worn woman bent over the stove in another and the stack of thin rolled up mattresses the boys pretended was a mountain in a third, would they be able to comprehend, she wondered.

Vibha descended into the daytime street and walked to the bus stop. Take an auto to the doctor's, the junior designer had urged, the firm will pay. But she didn't need a doctor. There wasn't any place in this city, frenetic with dreams and desperation, stretched thin and unrelenting beside the recoiling sea, that allowed for what she needed, what she'd had for a brief while, before the cleaner's return. The bus she boarded threaded its way through a web of streets narrow enough for her to reach out and touch the walls of the dwellings she passed. She looked in through the open windows at people crammed inside busily, frying batches of snacks, stringing flowers, rolling incense sticks. Oil fumes and sugary smells drifted out. Pots clanged, someone shouted, a hymn struggled in the jumble of noise. There was no peace.

Vibha alighted at the bottom of a street lined with stalls. A myriad of devotional offerings were on display in the flimsy cloth-and-bamboo structures – marigold garlands, incense sticks, sugar confections, votive offerings made of wax shaped like miniature houses, mortar boards, wedding rings, even coffins, a litany of wishes, desires, fears. A church, tall and grey, stood at the top. Walking towards it, Vibha was distracted by the statue of a woman in a glass-covered grotto. She wore diaphanous blue clothes, her head was covered like a married woman's. A man with showy, red-painted wounds lay in her arms. A cloying smell rose from the clump of incense sticks tucked in a mud-filled pot at the foot of the grotto. Vibha stared at the woman's face. She couldn't make out whether the creasing around the mouth was a grimace or a smile.

She wandered through the alleys radiating from the church, through village-like squares, old houses nudged into new shapes, large crosses erected at street corners, shanty-markets, handcarts of fried fish and bhajiya, clothes and trinkets, everyone buying, selling, begging, praying. A hawker trailing a large gaudy tin-sign painted with images of vermin – mosquitos, rats, bugs, roaches – all the same size and in similar menacing poses, attacking a hapless woman dressed in a tight pair of jeans, flowers dangling from her hair. Don't let vermin kill you, kill them first, ek naam sachcha Ram, god's name is true, he called out. People collected around him, buying the small, stoppered bottles of brown glass. How many rats will one bottle kill, someone asked. Sufficient to feed all village cats, pat came the reply, come on, buy, pay, move on, mix in dough balls, drip in drains, deadly to eat, deadly to drink, don't give it to your wife's lover, don't give it to your querulous neighbour, wash your hands carefully, come on, buy, pay, move on.

Vibha held out a ten-rupee note and received the brown bottle, unexpectedly warm to the touch.

I cleaned the bathroom with Dettol, the cleaner said, I washed all the bartan-bhande again, it is this bad weather, all kinds of bemari-shemari in the air, my wife came down with the same thing, mouth, anus both running, such chaos at home, thankfully my eldest daughter is fifteen, old enough to manage.

Vibha kept her eyes lowered, I am fine now, just need to take my medicine with warm water. Leaving him in the office space, she quickly stepped into the kitchen. The steel tumbler filled with steaming tea stood on the platform beside a plate of khari biscuits. She drew out the small brown bottle from her pocket and emptied a quarter of it into the tea, hastily stirring the boiling hot liquid with her little finger, scalding it.

She was washing her hands a second time with the disinfecting handwash when the cleaner entered. You want tea, he asked, I just made some. Vibha shook her head, no, no, still stomach issues. The cleaner picked up the steel tumbler, his hand shaking slightly and sipped the tea. I drank too much last night, not easy to live like this, my woman sick, my girls worried. Everything tastes bitter, he grimaced after a gulp, I know I should not drink but it is a hard life. Finishing the tea, he rose, too much work, too much worry, death is better than a poor man's life. Vibha's eyes widened. Involuntarily, she glanced at his face. It seemed paler and puffier than usual, his twisted eye red and moist. I am not feeling well, she said softly, I'll go home, please tell them when they come. Yes, okay, you want an auto, the cleaner asked, his hand on his stomach, his face perplexed at the discomfort there, I can get you one. No, no, don't bother, Vibha strode towards the door.

Vibha took the same bus as the day before. Again, she spent her day around the church. In the afternoon, she bought some fried fish, a chicken puff and a packet of sweet fugias and ate at the steps of the grotto, gazing up into the ambiguous face of the woman in blue. She had nothing further to do, except wait. Eventually, her phone buzzed with a series of messages. It was the junior designer. *Hey Vibs, how are you? Some bad news, Tiloki came down with severe alcohol poisoning. Dude chugged 2–3 bottles last night. Office a complete mess. Puke, diarrhea everywhere. We've called the cleaning crew to disinfect. Every1's WFH tomorrow. Ok*, Vibha tapped back, *I am ok now*. Tucking her phone in her backpack, she took out the bottle of rat poison and held it up. Rays of evening sun lit up the murky liquid within.

✣

Vibha emerged from her sleep slowly to the sound of groans and curses. She ground her teeth and braced herself for the day, and then she remembered.

She sprang up, her body felt light, easy, electric. Nothing mattered, neither the dim stagnant morning of Transy, nor the crowded bus with half-asleep women stacked together and the anxious haste of the city slowly coming awake. None of it touched her, in her mind she was already in the cool fragrant silent office, alone, unimpeded.

Vibha unlocked the frosted glass door and stepped in, her heart brimming, her mouth curved, her long cheeks creased. All was silent and still. She breathed in, slowly, deeply, quiveringly. Immediately, she gagged. Riding over the vaguely citrusy smell of the disinfectants used by the cleaning crew was the gravid, decay-laden, rotting-gut smell of sickness, like the reek of Transy's open drains and despair. Vibha staggered.

Robin McLean worked as a lawyer and then a potter in the woods of Alaska before turning to writing. Her first story collection, *Reptile House* (BOA, 2015), won the BOA Editions Fiction Prize and was noted as a best book of 2015 in *Paris Review*. Her debut novel, *Pity the Beast* (And Other Stories, 2021), was noted as the best book of fiction of 2021 in the *Guardian* and *Wall Street Journal*, and longlisted for the Reading the West Book Awards. Her second story collection, *Get 'em Young, Treat 'em Tough, Tell 'em Nothing* (And Other Stories, 2022), was an editors' choice in the *NYTimes*, and was longlisted for the Republic of Consciousness Prize. She was the 2023 visiting writer in the MFA program at the University of Montana. When not wandering the American Mountain West, she's found in Canada, on the edge of the Salish Sea.

Robin thinks that Vengeance (just a slot beyond its twin sister, Envy) is the most noxious emotion in the human repertoire. Beware this sparkling poison.

12

True Carnivores

ROBIN McLEAN

THEO STOOD ON his tiptoes on a chair facing the fridge. His chubby arm disappeared up to one striped shoulder, hunting inside the up-top freezer for Cherry Pops or Chocolate Twisters. He wore a tri-cornered hat with a chin strap. The counter was spotless but for a stack of sparklers and matches for later. Theo's hand explored deep internal regions, over forming ice cubes and crusted walls. Fog poured down his too-tight shorts, sank across his scraped-up knees and pooled on his toes.

Auntie watched him from the breakfast nook. She was tucked behind the half curtains, which were flowered, tied back with sashes by her sister, Theo's mother.

Sun soaked the kitchen windows, cast the breakfast nook in shadow: the table, Auntie's father's papers from the lawyer, her father in the urn by the wooden fruit bowl, the envelope with Auntie's plane ticket.

Sometimes Theo stopped, hugged the freezer door and listened for his mother, who was sucking up the living room with the vacuum, inhaling around couches, devouring at the feet of table legs, gulping pennies and game chips and plastic men too broken to bend for.

Auntie bit an orange to begin peeling it. She signed papers one by one. They'd stacked up for six months since the funeral, accounts consolidated, deeds transferred, the will all sorted out. She'd slept in the guest room. His estate was far larger than expected.

Citrus sprayed and Theo stopped to sniff. He stacked clam cakes in the bend of his arm, then bins marked chowder and frosty bags of lobster claws. He nibbled an edge of foil, then spat the foil out. The dog wagged and licked it up. Theo's fat belly was showing. He was a beautiful boy, so like his mother, so like herself.

You feed him too much, Auntie said at the funeral.

Her sister answered, *We'll miss you so much when you go*. Auntie set the pen down. She pushed the papers to the urn.

If she squinted hard, Theo at the fridge might be a one-armed boy: the victim of a shark bite or an amputation on doctor's orders. Who knows, she thought, where arms go when the mind wanders, when the retina is asked to stretch its object, to squeeze new options from rods and cones, to make suggestions to the optic nerve. If she squinted harder, he was the black-and-white boy in her father's baby pictures. Same nose, same eyes, same set of mouth.

Theo's face was red with cold and failure. Auntie licked her citrus fingers.

Out the window, the day was blue and fine, cooling finally. Birds ate at the feeder. Big ones chased the little ones off. Go away, little nothings. Find your own! They hopped onto the lawn for the next best answer. Telephone lines cut through branches. Birds clustered head-to-head or sat alone.

Then the chair teetered. Theo's tower leaned. The chair legs tipped out from under.

'Watch out!' Auntie called, but too late.

He held an ice cream sandwich aloft as he fell. His mother was too far off to hear the crash, the vacuum too loud. He lay on the tile. His eyes filled with tears as the mother-shape swooped in. He blinked them back when the shape was just Auntie.

'Don't tell,' he said.

'I wouldn't,' she said. She set the tri-cornered hat back on his head.

He ripped the wrapper. They sat on the floor and leaned against the fridge together. The vacuum roared up the front hall. Auntie yanked down his shirt to cover his belly. The gap in his teeth fit the ice cream at an angle. She'd tried to advise her sister. Theo must learn to fold his clothes, he must eat his peas, he must work harder at spelling.

You should make him brush better, she'd said once at the bathroom door.

They're only baby teeth, her sister had said, hand on the doorknob.

Theo had brushed in the mirror as they'd talked, then stripped for his bath, dancing on the bathmat shivering. Bubbles and water filled the tub.

I hate to see bad habits forming, she'd said, but the door had shut, locked.

What would we do without you! her sister had called over all that splashing. *These lawyers are such a handful! And you with your training!*

Let me in, Auntie said. She rapped on the wood. *Let me in.*

The fridge clicked and hummed against their backs.

'You look sad,' Theo said, and she said, 'Why would I be?' The vacuum was on the front stairs now, thumping up each carpeted runner, cord pulled to its limit, when the doorbell rang and the dog barked and ran to the door. The vacuum died. Bare feet thumped from the landing. 'Thank you, I'll take it,' her sister's voice said to yet another deliveryman, though the old house was so full already, closets, attics, mirrors, chairs.

Her husband blown to bits in his third foreign tour. Still, her sister had too much money.

Do you need so much? Auntie had said. *Aren't there better lessons to teach him?*

It's not a question of need, her sister said. *I'm a person who likes nice things.*

The vacuum resumed, a wand to the highest corners, gulping spiders and webs rebuilt since last time. Apologies mean nothing, prescribed, polite, and forgotten quickly. The ice cream sandwich lay melting. The cat licked it fast. The dog arrived and thumped his tail.

'I'm bored,' Theo said. 'Let's do something fun. Let's run or something.'

She stood and stretched. The slightest scent of toast lingered from the morning. She slid the toaster aside and found one fat crumb. She licked her finger, stabbed the crumb, then set it on her tongue. She turned a circle as the crumb dissolved. As a girl this had been her kitchen too.

At the nook, she tore up her plane ticket.

Once, when the sisters had been nine and ten, they'd wrestled over a locket on their mother's guest bed. *It's mine. No, it's mine. She gave it to me*, but who can say with so many years intervening, so many objects lost in linty corners, between mattress and box spring, drowned in the elbows of drains. Found is found. Possession being nine-tenths of the law, she'd learned. The locket was pewter. Her sister was taller and stronger, but was therefore too sure, therefore lacked imagination, therefore was less ready for the quicker hands from under the bed, from behind the door, for a patient will. She had won the locket on the guest bed but cried. Since fingernails cut. Since to gouge is startling. She had run then too, down the front stairway.

Get a backbone! her sister had called down the baninster, her face screwed up, leaning out too far over: *You nasty little thief!* Then the fall. Both legs broken. Father kneeling on the Persian runner. Blood.

Is she dead?

Not dead, her father said. *But I hope we've all learned a valuable lesson.*

The locket was given to her sister, compensation for months of convalescence.

It's not fair.

What's not fair is life, he'd said, kissing her sister's cheek.

Just look at history.

He was a lawyer himself and an amateur historian of early American pottery, shards and jugs, and a furniture restorer: spindle-backed chairs and wicker, which he viewed as the most marvellous of all the cottage crafts. *Think of the miracle*, he'd said at auctions. *Wicker starts as humble swamp grass. Soak the cane. Bend it. Shape it. Well-cared-for wicker will last for centuries.* Now, the vacuum was directly overhead, in the master bedroom, searching out specks. The cat cleaned its face with tongue and paw. The dog stood waiting.

Theo showed Auntie his bleeding elbow. She knew any mother would kiss it.

'Let's go, Theo,' Auntie said. 'Let's go for a little ride.'

✣

Her sister's bank was the Marblehead branch. The drive-through had closed early, but the lobby was open late. Theo ran around the lobby, dirtied the windows with sticky fingers as he stared out at the lobster boats, which bobbed in the harbour and docked, at the hands on board that threw ropes to hands onshore, at the hats and beards above those hands, at the pink sky, at gulls that tipped and balanced over boiling wakes. When he'd had enough of the view, Theo crawled between Auntie's legs. He punched calculator keys in the centre island.

The teller examined Auntie's paperwork, her sister's ID and account information, then excused herself to a supervisor.

The branch vice president emerged from a cubicle.

'Closing your account?' he said from the teller's window.

'Every one of them,' said Auntie. 'One cashier's check is fine.'

She sold her sister's minivan in Dover.

She traded for another, paid cash for the extra.

'I want green,' Theo said, and she pulled the thumb out of his mouth.

The newish green car had Alabama plates. It was the Fourth of July all the way to Pittsfield, chrysanthemum bombs and peony explosions. Roman candles ignited from front porches. Sulphur smoke drifted across the winding road.

'Can we call Mom?' he said, pointing at a rocket out the window.

Auntie dialled and handed the phone back. He said, 'It's ringing and ringing.'

The mountains were only low hills lit up in waxy blasts.

'The mountains get bigger.' She passed him a grinder wrapped in white paper.

'Great,' he said. 'I can't wait to see everything.'

He slept till Albany, which still fizzed and popped after midnight. Speed bumps woke Theo. Marble columns were red, white and blue. She parked at the porta-potties.

'There're fifty states, each with a capitol,' she said. 'Big decisions are hard.'

Theo said, 'I know all about that. Mom told me.'

The car steered by bunting-clad buildings and tricoloured fountains, past capital guards in glass-bubble booths, around roundabouts with bronze horses rearing, to horseshoe drives to spotlit mansions, then surged up ramps, through tolls, lanes merging. When sirens blasted, the car pulled over. An ambulance passed, then a squad car.

'Where are they going?' Theo said.

'To save someone,' Auntie said.

'A heart attack?'

'Probably just a broken leg.'

'Or robbers in ski masks robbing the bank?' He made a gun with his fingers. 'Stick 'em up, Auntie!'

She stuck her hands up, said, 'You watch too much TV.'

'I do!' He squealed, laughed and laughed.

The city went dark in the rearview mirror. It was much too late for robbing banks. More likely a fire, she thought. A stray bottle rocket. Or just one last cigarette in bed, the whole building going up like tinder, *Help us!* they are calling, good people with infants in upper windows, still believing real help is coming, not just sirens and expandable ladders. *Hold on, good people. We're almost there!*

They stopped for crepes in Columbus.

'Are we going to your house?' he said with strawberry syrup on his face.

She licked her thumb and rubbed the syrup. 'I sold my house.'

'Oh,' he said. 'Can we call home again?'

She dialled and handed the phone across the table. Theo listened. 'I think her phone's broken.'

✤

They found a Y in Fort Wayne that was air-conditioned. At Starved Rock, the grasshoppers were thick and spitting. Theo hopped behind them with a paper bag.

'Just one more, Auntie!' he said, and she said, 'Don't be greedy.' He lost his first tooth the next day in a burger in Joliet. He dropped it in a baggie. The roads toward St. Louis cut straight through fields that were flat and plowed east to westward. Towns announced themselves with stop signs and corn museums. The green was bigger than any blue bay, no lobster boats or buoys bobbing. They snuggled at night in queen-sized beds. She let him hold the clicker till 8.30. The pillowcases were musty but soft. He read the signs from county to county, Macon, Tazewell, his pronunciation perfect. Theo preferred the windows down past farms and tractors. Train tracks strung silos together. Deer twitched tails, ran and jumped wire fences, then stood under big black trees. They sang 'Mississippi' across the river, aimed at the Gateway Arch, which stood graceful and silver in the blue morning.

'What time did Mom say she'd meet us at the Arch?' Theo said on the off-ramp.

'She might already be up there.'

She glanced at her watch. He waved up at the tiny windows. They locked the car in a ten-dollar lot. They ran, swinging hands along the river, past the brewery and the stadium. The north leg shot up from concrete like a miracle. Bulky and clean cornered, it thinned as it rose, then reached for the south leg at the crotch, became it, then descended.

Theo ran with his baggie. 'I can't wait to show her. Chop chop, Auntie!' he called from the ticket window.

The guard let Theo push the elevator button. The capsule ticked sideways then upright as it rose. The observation deck was a tunnel of windows with seats for kneeling and looking out. He skated up the slippery floor. He examined every face.

'Where's Mom?'

'Has she ever let you down?' Auntie said.

He sat by the elevator. He'd already done the tour in the underground museum, studied the animatronic indigenous people. A school arrived for the morning history talk: 'Lewis and Clark: The Preparations'. 'St. Louis,' staff said. 'Where the captains found thirty hardy men and dropped boats in the river on President Jefferson's orders.'

The kids clapped and nodded. One asked for the bathroom.

The next group came pouring out of the elevator.

'Dragging boats over mountains,' staff said. 'Eating dog and parsnips... Clark and York, his slave, did not see eye-to-eye... Mosquitoes... Sacagawea and her papoose were minted on the modern quarter... Terrible bouts of diarrhoea.'

Kids grimaced. Staff handed out sew-on patches. The elevator doors were polished steel. Older kids came in the afternoon, high school. 'Syphilis,' staff said. 'Lewis only shot himself later... was out of his element in the city... Melancholia.'

'Suicide,' some kid said.

'What's parsnips?' said a girl in braids.

'It was like a thousand years ago,' said another. Sometimes it was quiet, sometimes swaying in big gusts.

Theo picked cheese off his sandwich. Mustard smeared his face. Auntie did not touch it. The river lay fat and brown. The elevator opened often. More schoolkids. He smoothed his hair every time.

'You look fine,' Auntie said. 'She'll think you look very handsome.'

Each time she dialled, and he listened, he said, 'We have the wrong number.'

Get a backbone, little girl, she thought. Stiffen your spine. Late afternoon, the sun dropped behind the tallest buildings. Auntie looked out one side, then the other. Illinois was flat and dull, belching smoke, the fields too far to see. Missouri was exactly the same but taller, prettier, made with better blueprints, glass and steel. Flags ringed the whole stadium. Wind caught the flags and flung them around. Below, people left work early. Walked dogs. Turned cartwheels. Kissed. Waved.

'I think I see Grandma!' called a girl who ran to the elevator. Theo covered his ears for the last of Napoleon, and Seward's Folly, maps, star charts and frontier medicine: purging pills to open bowels, lancets, forceps, gonorrhoeal syringes; Peruvian bark, laudanum; trinkets for the Indian Question; ammunition for thirty thousand, dinner, muskets, swivel cannons. '*To our inexpressible joy*,' staff said, 'Clark's words at seeing the Pacific... Smoked salmon all winter and Chinook squaws.'

Auntie ate when she could wait no longer, the bliss of the very hungry. The ham from the cooler was sweet and salty on buttered rye. Tomato seeds dripped in her lap.

Theo dropped pennies down the south-leg stairwell. He listened for clanging.

'You can't drop stuff down there,' staff said from behind him. Theo dropped a nickel. Staff stepped away.

'We'll be closing soon,' staff said to Auntie. The city was dark.

Often Father had set them on the front steps for punishment. *Face to face*, he'd said. *Hold hands.* Knees touching, he'd told them exactly what to say: *I love you*, one had said to get it over with.

I love you more, the other had said, picking her nose.

Again, he'd said. He drank from a sweaty glass delivered by Mother.

I love you so much I could kiss your face off. I love you so much I could eat you alive.

Try again, my dumplings. Do it right.

It's enough, Mother had said. *Let them stop.*

They need to learn a lesson. Right makes might.

Mother had died soon after. They'd lived on in the house, inherited by Father from his father, the second of five, who'd got the house when the eldest was lost at sea, some storm, the land purchased from a Quaker before that, who drank cider since wells could not be trusted, who had thirteen children since half died, farmwork, maize and oats, offspring of a whaling captain when lamps burned blubber, these mammals dragged port and starboard around Capes, Horn or Good Hope, back to Nantucket five years later, to repair leaks with tar, to start fires with flint, to teach the natives to pray, who knew his rights, who brought suit if a coop encroached on his tobacco.

Why does my sister get the house? she'd once asked him in the hospital.

Don't overthink it, he said. *She's got a kid. Rules are rules. Keep it in the family.*

In the elevator ticking down the leg of the Arch, staff gave Theo a lapel pin.

They walked by the stadium. The sky glowed above it but all else was black. A cheer rose up at some home run.

Theo ran.

'I want to see buffalo!' he called into the night sky.

✣

They went to story time at small libraries. They filled out patron questionnaires. They passed fences made of tires, wagon wheels, pallets turned upright. Wicker mannequins naked in dusty windows. Bikes in a mountain at a dried-up gas station, joints rusted black from rain, sale today = free. 'Should we take one?' Theo said, but there was so little room in the car. Water towers stood guard over every town, potbellied and swan-necked. Amish girls sweated over cheeses in low, shady roadside stands. They wore bonnets, aprons and sneakers. Mastless sailboats lay in cactus fields. Wicker chaise longues. Wicker rockers. Windsocks sucked north, south, east, west. 'Where are we going?' Theo said, leaning out the window.

'Everywhere,' she said. 'There are no rules for us.'

The continent was juniper, maple and cottonwood. Cattle in every colour. She baked birthday cakes in kitchenettes, folded in laundromats. He cried all night sometimes. He dropped each tooth into the baggie. 'Dear Tooth Fairy. Please don't take these yet.' When he was nine, they finally made it to Yellowstone. At Old Faithful, buffalo mingled between geysers. The rangers announced next eruptions. The earth was dry and cracked but burped and boiled.

'You'd cook in there in fractions of seconds!' Theo said.

He'd grown taller. He was getting very good at math. He wore a feathered headdress from the gift shop. The feathers danced in the sulphur updraft.

'But I'd catch you,' Auntie said, gripping the loop of his backpack.

'I said *you'd* cook. Not me.'

'I thought that was a figure of speech. *You'd cook* meaning *I'd cook*.'

'And if I was,' Theo said, 'what if you didn't?'

'The ranger would come,' she said. 'Pull you back from the pool just in time.'

'But if the ranger didn't?' he said. 'My skin would melt.'

'They would fix all that in the hospital,' she said. 'Skin grafts.'

'What's a skin graft?' he said.

'Patches of skin from someone else,' she said.

'My mom's skin?'

'Or mine.'

'What if the hospitals ran out of skin,' he said. 'Some bad guy stole it.'

'The doctor would give his own skin,' Auntie said. 'That's what doctors do.'

The pathways were wide enough for wheelchairs. He yelled every sign to practice his reading: 'Stay on path!' 'Noxious gases!' 'These animals may appear tame but they will gore you!' A wolf chased three bears in a meadow. Tourists surrounded a porcupine. They soaked in the Boiling River in shorts, near naked college girls giggling. Theo watched them roll in an eddy. A ranger came. He stood on the bank, looking down at the girls. He called out through his hands: bear on a kill just upriver. They all had to go. The college girls stood, dripping. The ranger supervised departure, helped the girls to their towels.

'Was there really a bear?' said Theo.

'Rangers don't lie.'

'Are you sure?'

'Yes.'

✥

Fourth of Julys cracked their eardrums every year: Niagara. The North Rim. He sat on the laps of Santas and Easter Bunnies. He trick-or-treated in safe-looking neighbourhoods. She kept a sewing machine in the trunk for costumes – a panda, a zebra, a lobster with red mitten claws. Fences made of stacked-up cars, smashed, rusted. Coyotes skewered on barbed wire. Sandlands, grasslands, salty seashores. She bought a new phone. They saw a cancan show in Virginia City, bought cowboy hats and boots, which Theo quickly grew out of. When he was ten, Auntie could borrow his biggest T-shirts.

'You'll be as tall as your dad,' she said. 'I knew him first, you know, your dad.' She wore his sweatshirts on cold mornings while the car warmed up, sniffed the dirty collars. 'We need to find a laundromat.'

'I don't remember him.'

⁂

They camped at Bannock and toured the old courthouse. She explained horse thieves and capital punishment, lynchings and Robin Hood. He could hardly believe it. Jupiter was low in the sky. They drank hot chocolate. They sent a card to his mother from Little Bighorn, where warriors had crouched behind rocks with arrows. Theo studied the address, dropped the card in the slot.

'Are we bankers or something?' he said, since they did business at banks in various states. She explained safe deposit boxes, hedge funds, offshore accounts, white-collar crime. She kept cash in a sack beneath the spare in the trunk. She kept the car keys no matter how much he begged to hold them. They drove up into the mountains. They turned in at every Lewis and Clark pullout, where the Corps of Discovery had almost starved, where the Corps of Discovery had gone without water, where the Corps of Discovery had trudged through chest-deep snow behind their Shoshone guide, Old Toby.

'How could they really trust him?' Theo said on a sandy bank. He kicked a charred log from some old fire.

'They roasted the horses one by one.'

He got back in the car.

They camped on the Lolo. Trees drowned out highway noises. The ridges stood steep and dark. The fire was warm and good. Wind moved only the top branches.

'Sacagawea saved them, yes,' Auntie said. 'But she was kidnapped as a girl.'

'I know,' Theo said. 'We're kidnappers. Smallpox spreaders.' Theo cooked a hot dog on a stick.

'When you were little,' Theo said, 'who was the faster? You or Mom?'

'I was faster.'

'But,' he said, 'she broke both legs once.'

'Yes. But I was faster even before that.'

The trees were black and close over the tent. The moon tipped on the east ridge.

'My mom's tuna casserole's really good.'

'My tuna casserole's excellent too. I'll make it at the next motel.'

The fire snapped with Theo's grease.

'My mom's tuna casserole is the best,' he said. 'No one can beat it.'

A rabbit appeared in the firelight, big ears turning. 'Do we have enough money?' he said.

'Your mother made sure we had plenty.'

'What if the bank with our money caught fire?'

'It's in a computer,' she said. 'Not a building.'

'What if the computer got a virus?'

'They'd fix it.'

'What if the tech guys caught the Plague?' he said. 'Spitting up blood. Arms falling off.' Bats banked and dipped around the smoke.

'Tech guys would come from the next town over.'

His hot dog had split down the side. He pried it onto the bun. 'What if every town got the Plague,' he said. 'All America. Corpses all over.'

'They'd fly helicopters in from Canada,' she said. 'Full of tech guys.'

'What if the whole world got the Plague?'

He ate. Coyotes yipped. The moon hoisted over the ridge and stood there.

'What's that weird pot in the trunk?' he said. 'Under all those papers?'

'It's an urn, not a pot,' she said. 'Don't touch it.'

Wicker lampstands at yard sales. Wicker baskets at farmer's markets brimming with tomatoes, onions, piles of beans. 'The cane is hand-twisted,' she explained, tricoloured, her father's favourite, some empty, or holey, or eaten, or crushed, or burned. Fences were made of license plates or skies nailed to split rail. Grassy Knolls, Trails of Tears, bison and missile ranges, golden roller coasters in the desert. He saved his allowance in a sock. She peeked out a steel restroom door to watch him hide the sock in the trunk, beneath the sack of cash, beneath the spare, smoky breath at his mouth. He hogged the covers every night, stacked all the pillows behind him. He thinned and ate and grew in sudden growth spurts. He paid close attention to the dials and pedals, sat behind the steering wheel when Auntie pumped gas. He learned to pump gas. He learned to use the jack, fit the lug wrench, change a tire. When he was twelve, they began to shop in men's sections. His voice was cracking. She bought him deodorant.

'I use deodorant too,' she said. 'We have a lot in common.'

He dropped the drugstore bag on the bed. He peeled his T-shirt off in the motel mirror. His shoulders had widened. Muscles were forming. He snapped off the deodorant cap, set it on the TV, raised his elbow to his ear, rolled the deodorant stick across his armpit, crushing and re-crushing each crinkled hair. She lay back on the bed, looked up his beautiful spine, the low spots between his ribs, the golden fuzz still on his nape.

'What else do we have in common?' he said. 'I can't think of anything.'

The letters to Santa finally stopped. He brushed his teeth with the door shut. One New Year's Eve, they watched fireworks in Anchorage: dandelions bursting up and gone in the jet stream. They'd taken the ferry from Bellingham to avoid customs, driven up the ramp and parked on the car deck. They slept on the upper deck under heaters. 'Fun?' she said, and he said, 'Fun,' as the ferry slipped up past Canada, fish camps and trawlers. Mountains spiralled to hanging glaciers, clouds swirling round the highest peaks. In Fairbanks, the motel pool was glassed in. He carried her around the no-running area. She kicked in his arms, 'Theo! Theo!' before he tossed her in the deep end. She floated by the drain, let chlorine soak into her. She had had no idea such joy existed.

At the Grand Canyon he said, 'I want to see Thomas Jefferson.'

They camped at Mount Rushmore, but that wasn't good enough. In North Dakota, they were stopped at a roadblock. The trooper flashed a flashlight in the window.

'Where are you from?' said the trooper.

'Bangor, Ohio,' Auntie said. 'What's going on, officer?'

'I can't give details,' said the trooper. 'Just tell your son not to stare.'

Theo blinked in the flashlight.

'She's not my mother,' Theo said, but the trooper was already at the next car.

✣

He slept with the TV clicker. Animal shows looped all night. Experts murmured as insects swarmed. Every gazelle ran for its life. He lay on bathmats, clicked from station to station, chewed vitamins slowly. 'I'm big enough for my own bed.' She said she'd think hard about it. Reporters appeared in every country, diseased frogs in disputed areas, elephants killed for ivory trinkets. Turtles got inoculations, fish needed decontamination. Storms rolled around the globe on all-night weather, balled up in polar and equatorial regions. El Niños, nor'easters, typhoons. Ships bobbed, then capsized. Penguins were marooned on desert islands. He watched with the sound off as seals were tossed and smashed by flukes. Dictators shot parliamentarians. Lions and orcas always won.

'I love you more than anyone,' she said in a sleeping bag.

'Could we go to a movie?' Theo said. 'Or bowling?'

VACANCY flashed in green or pink. 'We're from Boston, Minnesota,' she told a waitress. 'Portland, Kentucky,' she told another. 'Sisters, Texas.' 'York, Arizona.'

'You always get it wrong,' he said. He chewed saltwater taffy, pulled it from between his teeth. Pig roasts, salmon derbies, Six Flags, chocolate factories, dairy farms, abandoned ski jumps, mansions passed over by Sherman, log cabins, volcanoes. Once, she saw Theo's picture on a milk carton, then in a post office in Louisville, then on LateNite FBI, but the photos were unrecognisable now, a much younger boy, a different mood. Her own face, set at the bottom of the screen, had been smooth-skinned then, the beginnings of the lopsided smile. They stayed west and south, steered clear of the north Atlantic. It was so easy, so much empty space. She nipped at night from a flask. Her skin grew dry, not enough aloe in all the world. And her back.

He walked on her spine, her face in the motel

carpets, but only if she begged him, then later only if she let him drive.

'But you're only thirteen.'

'Almost fourteen.'

She slept with the keys at night. In St. Paul she lost him at a disco skate, found him with a girl in slush and fog, the Zamboni driver. They found old phone booths all over, favourites in Abilene and at Devil's Tower. He parked and lay on the minivan roof. She pulled the glass doors shut behind her. He rolled his eyes to the stars, cold steel on his back. A satellite flew over and he watched it watching everything everywhere.

'What is love anyway?' he said. 'What does *love* mean?'

She pointed at her ear, mouthed *Can't hear you.* Handsets were sliced away, phone books ripped up for toilet paper, but dials still spun easy on the finger everywhere.

'I should look it up,' he said. 'My nice dictionary is in the backseat.'

She fumbled to dial.

'What will you say if she ever answers?' He echoed off cliffs and billboards.

She didn't say what she would say: 'I win, I win, I win.'

At Monticello they arrived for a small first ever! festival, strolled a pop-up street called Mulberry Row, tents and booths of weavers, spinners, and pewter-pourers. They stood at velvet cords that said do not enter. They watched ponies drink at hollowed logs. She tried raccoon caps from a man in buckskin. Theo was too old for them now. The smith showed him how to swing the hammer, how gravity must take the weight so as not to overtax the wrist and shoulder, since a smith must swing it for many long years, he said, to feed his family, an entire lifetime shoeing horses, outfitting soldiers in case the nation, at any moment, should be called to war.

'How can that rock be burning?' Theo said, staring at the coal. 'It just does,' the smith said, chewing gum.

'Are you supposed to be a slave?' Theo said.

'Well,' said the smith. A little man walked in in velvet, a red wig, powdery face.

'Fine day,' said the wigged man in a British accent. The smith bowed. 'Good day, sir.'

Theo said, 'You're supposed to be Jefferson?'

'That I am,' said the man. 'And you must be a young patriot.'

'I learned all about you in the visitor centre.'

'Very fine,' said the man. 'A boy who loves his country.'

'And what you did to Sally.' Theo stepped forward very tall. 'I saw the video.'

'Knowledge is good,' said the man, backing out. 'Power is complicated.'

The man strolled up the Row waving at the craftspeople in leather aprons on their porches. Theo followed, then Auntie. The man slid through a staff-only door.

'Is there no one who is not polluted?' said Theo on the way to Appomattox. 'I want to go to Canada!'

They bought a blue convertible in Las Vegas to cheer him up. Traded for yellow in Valley Forge, then a pickup with a topper in Silver City, a stick shift.

'I guess I'm back to pilot again,' she said. 'Since you don't know the clutch yet.'

Theo took the keys from the salesman and headed for the truck.

'Watch me.'

⁂

They joined a funeral motorcade in Provo. The graveyard was on a red rock hill with a picket fence. People held black umbrellas. They parked. Someone waved them over.

'Thanks for coming,' one woman said.

'Such a loss,' Auntie said. 'I'm so sorry.'

They declined the invitation to the wake. With the family gone, they sat in the front row. The backhoe stood ready in the distance. The afternoon cooled.

'We don't belong here,' Theo said. 'Mormons.'

'People are people,' she said. 'Try to be open-minded.'

Prairie dogs burrowed between graves. RATTLESNAKE signs hung on the fence.

'John F. Kennedy cheated on his wife,' he said. 'The lunar landing was a fake.'

'They couldn't fake a thing as big as that,' she said.

'Wake up, sister!' he said. 'Hollywood! Moon rocks made from Styrofoam.'

'Don't call me sister,' she said. 'And where's my urn, by the way.'

'You get the urn,' he said, 'when I get the address.'

'This is puberty,' she said. 'That urn's my property.'

He stood at the grave. 'What if she wonders how tall I am?' he said. 'What if she wonders if I learned to read right? If I'm happy. If I'm good at all.'

'You see how soft you are?' she said.

'Was it Maine? Rhode Island?' he said. 'I see boats. A harbour. It's gotten foggy.'

'I'm worried about you,' she said. He kicked some roses in the hole.

'I know where the money is,' he said. 'I know how to get it.'

'You may think you know.'

'I want the address.'

'It's no use discussing locations,' Auntie said. 'Your mother's dead.'

Theo dropped out of sight. His sneakers gonged the coffin. The flashlight died that night. She made a tent of some chairs and a blanket. She threw a coat down. He threw it back. The air was full of dirt and salt. She coughed and sneezed. She was getting stiff, arthritis. The stars spun around.

'Let's do something fun,' she said. 'Blue whales? Redwoods? Dinosaur fossils?'

She bought passports in an alley in Salt Lake City. He didn't speak for 2,000 miles.

The CBC played ragtime all through Saskatchewan: Saskatoon, Prince Albert, Flin Flon. Going north, the land turned from brown to green to red to white. They left the pickup at Split Lake and chartered a plane, small and bumpy, that landed in Churchill. They stood in a line. She bought polar bear tickets for the next morning.

At the restaurant, he ordered lobster, small and red on a very large plate. Its claws were pinned with wedges, arms enclosing a crock of hot butter. He ripped an arm out. When he twisted the thumb from its sheave, the cartilage stood out naked and translucent. He ripped the other arm. Silty juice flowed down his wrist. He licked it. He cracked the shell with his teeth, dug in fissures with his fingers, smashed the shell with the small hammer provided. Pried, twisted, hacked, then slurped. He chewed with his mouth wide open, molars crushing muscle, tongue sliding in and out.

She set her fork down. 'Stop it,' she said, and he said, 'Stop it.' He ripped the spider legs out, one to ten, then two antennae, then plucked the eyes, and set them both beady on her plate.

He tore the lobster in half. An orange pile fell from the ragged sinew of the tail. He spooned the pile and gobbled orange.

'You're grotesque,' she said. 'This is not how I raised you.'

'*You're grotesque*,' he said.

He cut the tail open with the scissors provided, then folded back the ribbed skin. How many times had it molted? Zipped down the front to wriggle it out. How many shells lay just offshore and empty? Under lighthouse beams for decades, skidding thoughtless over waves, over matings and hatchings. Theo set down the scissors. The whole restaurant was eating. No one was watching. The tail meat curled in his hand, bashful, shy, ready to pump up and down and swim away.

'A bottom dweller,' he said. 'A carrion eater.'

He turned the tail over. A green vein ran the length of the underside. He inserted his finger, ripped the vein out, dangled it high over his open mouth. Dropped the vein in.

✣

Morning, the hall was long and dark to the lobby, past the coffee maker. A ten-foot bear stood opposite the brochure rack. Theo wore a bandanna on his head. He pushed by the bear and out the door into the night-black northern morning.

The Polar Stalker was a glass-roofed vehicle with extra-wide tracks designed for snow. They shivered and breathed diesel as they stood in line with tickets, then climbed the stairs through the narrow door. Heaters blasted at the boot line. The guide had pimples, said he'd never been out of Manitoba. Theo sat by a window. She slid in behind him. She offered a muffin. He snapped the window latch, flung the muffin.

'Don't feed the wildlife,' said the guide, but grinned.

It was a nine-mile loop to Hudson Bay. The Polar Stalker rolled and bucked over tundra. The sun lay stubborn below the horizon.

'Churchill has more polar bears than anywhere,' droned the guide as the lights of town grew smaller. 'We are on a migrational path.' The sky was full of stars. The Bay was the nothing in the distance. The Stalker rumbled toward it. Clusters of light bobbed and wagged toward the Stalker. 'Kids on the way to school,' said the guide, as snowmobiles raced by in packs of threes or fours behind headlights, kids bundled behind the drivers, coats and scarves whipping and snapping in the last efforts of the moon. Auntie slept. When she woke, the land had ended and the Bay begun. The sun was starting gold on the water. Birds bobbed. Seal heads appeared and disappeared.

'You see "bears" all over,' said the guide. 'Yellowstone. Jasper. Everywhere, like mice, in those low-latitude places.' The Stalker rolled on along the shore. 'But what you see there are just grizzlies and black bears. Omnivores. Meaning they'll eat anything: berries, roots, trash. Like dogs or goats, what have you, okay, but that's not a real bear.'

Theo's face was so young, listening. She set her eyes on the side of it, her mitten on his shoulder. He swatted her hand away. 'The polar bear is a real bear, the King of Bears,' said the guide. 'He stalks you. Eats meat only. Will drag your kid off. A true carnivore.'

Theo sat up, searched the tundra.

'Where are all the bears?' someone said in the back.

'Polar bear sightings are not guaranteed,' the guide said, monotonous and calm.

The Stalker rolled along the shore. Woodpiles littered the beach. Rocks lay in lines pinned with icy webbing. The Stalker idled near promising air holes, trundled on. When town reappeared, the Stalker aimed toward a gift shop.

'I'm sorry,' she said over his shoulder. 'I wish we'd seen at least one bear.'

'There are no bears.'

'We just hit an off day.'

'The ice is melting,' he said.

'We'll retake the tour.'

'They all sank.'

'But there are islands,' she said. 'There are Greenpeace ships.' The Polar Stalker parked, passengers disembarked.

'The bears drowned,' he said. 'They're all dead.'

At the Stalker office, Theo whispered with the guide at the reservations counter. Auntie found the restrooms. When she came out, Theo and the guide were gone. She headed back through the town toward the motel, past houses crouched on tiny lots, facing any way they wanted, plywood, plastic flowers sprouting in the snow, each with dogs on chains. The urn might be anywhere.

She passed groups of trick-or-treating families. 'I'd

forgotten,' she told a mother with a very small soldier. 'Halloween.' She merged with the crowd door-to-door. Kids ran ahead with their candy sacks open. Moms hustled behind. Men stood with rifles at street ends, in the glow of flares at the edge of the tundra, the town's perimeter. They wore camouflage parkas, spoke into walkie-talkies. She stared out at the land behind the flares.

'Bears,' a man called to her.

She nodded, looked around at the families. 'Where's your kid?' said a mom.

'I'm going to find him now.'

'What's his name?'

When Auntie said it, the woman turned quick, called 'Theo!' between her gloves.

They all stopped and called out. The women in booming voices. The kids in costume dropped their candy, screaming it. The men in flares yelled it, then searched through binoculars, jumped on snow machines ready to ride.

'Theo! Theo! Theo!' they called. Like a mother should.

Her face burned. Her mittens covered her exposed ears. Where had her hat gone? No trees, no road signs, no road. She thought of home, the Atlantic, where trees were giants leaning deep into well-paved streets. Leaves were red this time of year, had only just begun to fall and rot. Phone lines tunnelled through limbs, union men trimmed them. Squirrels ran the tightropes, leaped from branch to knot of fungus growing, fought for nuts to stuff in nests. If a dead one fell and lay in the street, kids called other kids over to poke the skull with sticks, to grimace at the seepage, to jump back if the dead thing moved.

She waved them on. He's at the motel. The families kept on calling as she ran.

The snow was stiff and noisy underfoot. Dusk, the far-out flat was still visible. Nothing. White reflected any star. Hudson Bay was just a gray line forever. Snow machines raced out in search of the missing boy, the motors eaten by the wind.

The motel was all lit up. She did not unzip in the lobby. She turned a circle by the bear that seemed to watch the TV across the room. A cooking show, some casserole. When Theo appeared down the hall, he was taller now than the vending machine, peanuts and cookies.

'Theo,' she said. He didn't turn. He pounded the machine with his fist. He kicked the machine then searched the slot at the bottom, stuffed a packet in his coat, someone else's, green with a stripe down the arm. He disappeared down the hall, toward the service entrance.

She sat with the bear. Its shaggy head touched the

ceiling, bullet-shaped, pure white. She could see no bullet hole. Dead, yes, but with front paws sprawled as if for embrace, web-footed, claws taller than her thumbs. A slick black tongue lolled between incisors, yellowing. The eyes were not bad eyes. Hungry. Surprised by sudden death.

She borrowed a flashlight from the night clerk. She slid the truck keys across the counter. 'Please give these keys to that boy I'm with.'

The fluorescent bulb blinked on the fax machine.

'To your son?' The clerk swept the keys into a drawer.

'Just the boy,' said Auntie. 'He's someone else's son.'

She wrote an address on a motel pad. The night clerk leaned to see it, some upside-down place way down south.

'This too,' Auntie said, almost passed it over, pulled the pad back only when the night clerk reached. She ripped the top page off, balled it up and took it with her as she headed for the door.

'Be careful,' said the night clerk. 'Don't walk too far. Bears are out.'

But she wanted to walk far, to meet a bear ten feet tall, a living one, shake hands.

Auntie stepped into the window-lit town and out of it. Not one fence for a million miles. She pulled her mittens off, unzipped her coat, unwound her scarf and dropped it. Maybe it would reunite with the hat. She tottered out into the tundra, followed some snow machine tracks. They were still calling out. She should tell them to stop.

She walked. It had been so long since she'd just gone walking.

The Bay was not so far.

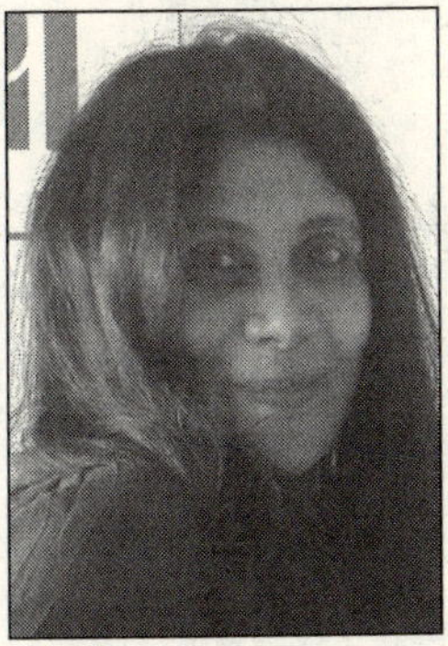

Shinie Antony is a writer and editor based in Bengaluru. Her novels include *Eden Abandoned: The Story of Lilith*, *Can't* and *The Girl Who Couldn't Love*. Her short-story collections include *Barefoot and Pregnant* and *The Orphanage for Words*. She has put together the anthologies *Boo*, *Why We Don't Talk* and *An Unsuitable Woman*; and co-edited the anthology *exObjects: The Art of Holding On, Letting Go* with A.T. Boyle. Shinie is the founder of the Bangalore Literature Festival and festival director of the Bengaluru Poetry Festival. Her story 'A Dog's Death' won the Commonwealth Short Story Prize for the Asia region in 2002.

Revenge, to this author, is a twist in the tale, a stab in the back, all enemies ash in an urn.

13

This Little Heart of Mine

SHINIE ANTONY

THIS IS WHAT I'm thinking in the middle of the rape. This is not rape. This is consensual. He is my boyfriend. I have known him for months, haven't I?

No, you haven't. He is a stranger who has broken into your home and brutally attacked you in your sleep. There's blood sticky on your temple and one of your teeth is loose.

My head is banging against the wall behind my bed. I'm trying my best to pretend this is just sex with someone I love madly. I will my body to turn limp, pliant. Because I don't want to die. That possibility has just occurred to me.

I have been a good girl all my life. Not good so much as anonymous – hard to pick even two people who'd notice if I shaved off my hair. The guys I liked liked other girls, so there was no trouble maintaining my 'goodness'. Sex happened in safe, far-off places, in books and films, with one bare shoulder peeping out from a sheet, the tip of a pink tongue between white teeth.

A slapping noise as he readjusts his grip – how slippery we are! His whole body is clasping my whole body, his chin digs into my cheek. I feel small, made of nits. When I inhale, I exhale jerkily all over his face. I can't even breathe correctly! This makes me anxious, and I tell myself this is only a B-grade film, what I watched with my mother in an endless adolescence – just her and me and the over-coloured claustrophobic TV. I am the heroine, and the hero will be here any minute, fighting traffic and the hostel warden, to rescue me just in time... No, no, my brain cuts me off, no saviour is lurking around this late, looking for an idiot to rescue.

I am going to die, this is death, this is my death, I am turning into my own ghost. My brain chants: Make him another man, make him someone else, make him... *he*?

I tell me it is he till I believe me. My feet flop sideways and fists unfurl. Just thinking of *this* man as *that* man makes my armpits feel like a doll's – dry, deo-scented. I feel disoriented; where am I? My bed or his? I shut my eyes in the dark and in the darker dark the large flowers of my sheet begin to vanish. I feel blue stripes from another sheet. He is here, can you believe that? Him from my class.

Him I so liked from the day he wandered late into class and sat next to me because I was sitting closest to the door. I remember how my stomach had contracted before completely liquefying. I had sat there next to him, trying to contain a me that was turning into the rapids.

And here he is, backlit. Stealthy and cute. One day we will giggle over this unorthodox night. I will punch him lightly on his chest and say, 'You!'

The man is holding my thighs apart. I let them fall like dead wings. I cup his face tenderly and decide it is time for speech. Because one of the scariest things ever since this began is the silence. But the words I drag out, they start to leak from holes in my neck... Like gargoyles that spit water, accursed to forever glug but simply not swallow, stone throats open both ends. I sense a change in him at my failed attempt to speak, a waiting, wary. I tentatively stroke his back. Ignoring the sweat on his back, my fingers push up and down; a squeak as my fingers go upstream on his spine. A muscle flexes. His or mine, don't know. He grunts.

I say again with dry lips, 'I love you.' This time the words screech out like a train from a tunnel.

Is he laughing? His chest, pressed hard against me, zigzags. He pinches my lip between his fingers. Then he says with a southern accent, 'Girl only.' I listen with utmost care as he speaks; he is disappointed (my brain notes for later reference) but in a pleased way. I had disappointed him just the way he wanted to be disappointed.

My body absorbs his voice. It fills me up like an empty bottle inside a stream, the glug of *girlonlygirlonly*.

He wraps his hand round my neck. I close my eyes. He doesn't move. He continues to not move. 'W... what?' I force myself to say. If he has me classified as an upper-class English-speaking type, then I want him to feel a part of that world, an 'our' world.

He makes an incoherent sound between panting and a consonant.

'What?' I ask again. For the shape of the last few minutes is about to change, I'm slyly, secretly aware. I am in on a future, mine only if he chooses. He softens within me, his breath gentling before his body does. I'm dazed by the speed of him lifting off me. Like a lorry rolled off me. My heart is not beating. It had stopped beating the moment I had come awake with a hand clamped over my mouth.

He lies to the side, his face away from me.

Can I switch on the light?

No reply. Because, I will realize later, I have not said these words in a way another person other than me can hear. When I tremble an arm across to reach the light switch, he makes a protesting noise and I stop my hand midway.

He is moving, but not towards me. There are rustling noises and I'm guessing (without consciously doing so) he is picking his clothes. There is a moment in the dark when I know he is looking at me. I lie docile. I don't want to tense up again. Then he is gone. Just like he had come. Abruptly.

In the darkness, straining my ears, I cannot believe he is gone. About an hour later I spasm head to toe. My heart starts to beat again, a muffled thud, tentative, as if in a chest nearby, not mine. With great effort I slide to the end of the bed. My feet when I finally push them out of bed refuse to touch the floor. They dangle.

In bathroom with the light on, but I don't remember the mirror.

❖

The next day, my roommate is back around 10 a.m. and she takes me to the campus police station. They write down what I say. Give me tea and water. There is a doctor for my body and a doctor for my mind. This has, they keep saying, never happened in the campus before. Never.

I allow myself to be patted and prodded. A gynaecologist with gloved hands fades in and out. Swabs and lab reports. We are officially in rape territory. I don't shut my eyes against the camera flash.

I am treated with hush. With a cat-pawed, candle-lit kindness. Yes, I sigh by evening, I know who it is. They catch hold of him by midnight. I don't have to see him. I give them the name and they find him in his room. Of course, he denies it. He provides alibi. He was with a professor's wife, he said, but no one believes him. Lying to get out of the rape charge, they scoff.

He is suspended. He is expelled. He is arrested. He is jailed. His rich parents fly in from abroad to hire lawyers, bribe whoever and hold his hand. They will jet him from judicial custody straight back to their kingdom, the little crown prince.

I sit on the swing in my mother's house and try to prise apart all the men inside my head into separate men, but they run into each other, sticky mucous. I'm sipping coke with a straw. It is cold and tingly down my throat. Every part of me must be reclaimed. I am a reclamation project. I shut my eyes when I hear my mother's footsteps, pretending to sleep so she can watch me with that nameless expression.

Why was the door open? Did I encourage this guy? I must have done so. Think, think... You are too quiet, she had said out of the blue when I was grappling with the food she claims I'd been fond of as a child. My lack of reply seemed to satisfy her; I had proved her right. If I had been loud, verbose, saying what came to my mind, a talker and a yeller, all the bad luck headed my way would have slunk away. When I was a child, she says, she had taken me to a speech therapist and even psychic healers. To make me talk.

'You read too much' was her real complaint. My vocabulary, some teachers have said to her, was beyond my years. I was too... articulate. She had a mother's distrust of all the words I was thinking but not saying.

When she reached the principal's office, I'd seen her before she saw me, before she could arrange her face. She had to hear the details, which she did as her motherly duty. We never spoke of it. Between us were detailed queries about an aunt's chemo, passport renewal and her bunions – she may need an operation as two toes now overlapped, but where was the time? I woke up to noises in the kitchen; she always got up early to cook. Chopping, grating, stirring – and running through it all the angry hum of her soul.

If there is one thing she had done ever since she had me, the one thing she dedicated her life to, it was guarding my virtue. Like a lone soldier entrusted with an entire contentious border, she anxiously waited for just such an invasion. A war she prepared all her life to lose. A war she had now lost.

In the evenings we both sat reading, turning the page when we became aware of how long it had been since we turned a page. When her phone rang, she went out of the room to take the call. My phone was with her. It had been confiscated for my own good. Her moods allowed for a burst of optimism now and then, when she would pick up my chin, study my face in all angles and declare me not bad-looking.

⚘

After he sat next to me in class that first day, he never did again. If you asked him, he wouldn't have known my name. Now he does. I can see him study his fingernails each time they show him close-ups of my scratches. Why did she say that, he is thinking. Why did I say that, I am thinking. Have I gone mental, is this limerence, or PTSD as everyone claims? He asked to meet me, a request denied by all around me. The professor's wife has spoken to the police, swearing she had been with him that night. But then everyone remembers me clearly. Retching on that plastic chair.

My mind is never on the stranger of that night, fracturing my wrist and giving me a concussion. His hiss at not being able to complete the act. He is no one.

⚘

That day I had studied him shyly all through the lecture. Denim knees, the blunt nails so close to my own black painted ones. He smelled of diesel, one a.m. texts and late assignments. When the class ended, I had turned to him, my heart a dancefloor, summoning up all my braveries and spoken as loudly and clearly as I could. Hello, I said. I saw his gaze fall away. Then he was off, loping away to a bunch of seniors looming by the door. Bro, he said to them. Bro, they said to him.

I sat still, my hello cawing loudly back at me.

Publication History

True Carnivores

'True Carnivores' is reproduced here with permission of And Other Stories after its first publication in *Get 'em Young, Treat 'em Tough, Tell 'em Nothing*.

Following

'Following', published by Jacaranda Books Arts Music Limited in *Speak Gigantular*, 2016. © Irenosen Okojie, 2016.

Three Days in Hong Kong

From *The Carnal Fugues*, published by Puncher & Wattmann, Australia, in October 2023.

The Man Who Types

Adapted from *The Typing Man*, published in 2013.

When Carl's Café Closed Its Door on Me

Reproduced in arrangement with HarperCollins Publishers India Private Limited from the book *This Is How It Took Place* by Rudrakshi Bhattacharjee.